Terror in Florida

Roy MacGregor

M&S

An M&S Paperback Original from
McClelland & Stewart Inc.
The Canadian Publishers

An M&S Paperback Original from
McClelland & Stewart Inc.

Canadian Cataloguing in Publication Data
MacGregor, Roy, 1948–
    Terror in Florida

(The Screech Owls series; 6)
ISBN 0-7710-5616-8

I. Title. II. Series: MacGregor, Roy, 1948–   .
The Screech Owls series; 6.

PS8575.G84T47 1997   jC813'.54   C97-932164-6
PZ7.M233Te 1997

Cover illustration by Gregory C. Banning
Typesetting by M&S, Toronto

Printed and bound in Canada

McClelland & Stewart Inc.
The Canadian Publishers
481 University Avenue
Toronto, Ontario
M5G 2E9

  1 2 3 4 5   01 00 99 98 97

ACKNOWLEDGEMENTS

The author is grateful to Doug Gibson, who thought up this series, and to Alex Schultz, who pulls it off.

1

TRAVIS LINDSAY HAD TWO DREAMS THAT KEPT coming back to him, time and time again. In the first, he was at his grandparents' cottage and something had happened to the water. He would wake in the morning and the lake would be entirely dry but for the odd pool of water and a lot of slippery mud, as if somebody had pulled out a big rubber bathtub plug in the middle of the lake. Instead of snorkelling around the surface with his rubber flippers and mask, he was now able to roam the lake bottom on foot, collecting lost lures and finding out, for once, just how big the trout were.

Travis's second dream was about winter vanishing. In Travis's home town, there came a time every late February or early March, when, suddenly, everyone grew sick and tired of winter — even young hockey players like Travis and the rest of the Screech Owls. You got up one morning and, instead of looking forward to practice or a tournament on the weekend, you started looking forward to spring: the first robin, the first sound of flowing water, the first smell of earth wafting up through the snow, the first day you could run out of the house without a winter jacket and boots.

In the dream where winter went away, it always happened instantly. Travis would wake up – at least he'd *dream* he had woken up – and there would be birds in the trees and the smell of manure being spread in the farm fields at the edge of town, and Wayne Nishikawa, *Nish*, would be firing pebbles at his window and shouting for him to come out and play.

This time, however, Travis's end-of-winter dream was different. It was *really* happening! And not just to Travis, but to Nish – snoring away in the seat beside him – and Data, up a row, and Lars, Jenny, Dmitri, Andy, Gordie, Jesse, Derek, Willie, Jeremy, even Sarah Cuthbertson, two seats back and playing hearts with Wilson and Fahd and the Owls' newest player, Simon Milliken. Simon was the smallest player on the team – smaller even than Travis, who was finally going through a growth spurt – and was a bit puck-shy. Nish had pounced on Simon's weakness, tagging him with a dreadful nickname – "Chicken Milliken" – that had, unfortunately, stuck. Fortunately, Nish was sound asleep; otherwise he might have been hounding poor Simon at this very moment.

The Screech Owls filled a school bus, each player allotted an entire seat to him or herself so they could all stretch out and sleep. Even old Muck was on board, in the front seat, the big coach so deep in a thick book that Travis wondered if he even realized they had left Canada and were almost halfway to Florida. *Halfway to summer! Halfway to Disney World!*

With Mr. Dillinger, the team manager, driving, the Owls had left for Florida at the beginning of the March school break. And though Travis knew it was still March on the calendar, it sure didn't feel like it. Every few hours it seemed like a whole month had passed. Winter was peeling away. They could now see grass in the fields!

Behind the rented school bus – slow, noisy, and uncomfortable, but cheap, Muck said – there were parents' cars and Mr. and Mrs. Cuthbertson's Winnebago, and the two assistant coaches, Barry and Ty, in the rented van filled to the brim with hockey and camping equipment. Camping, Muck had argued, was another way to save them money.

They were off to the Spring Break Tournament, Peewee Division II, with games in Orlando and Lakeland, Florida, with special three-day passes to Disney World and – if they made it to the finals – a chance to play for the championship in the magnificent Ice Palace, home rink of the NHL's Tampa Bay Lightning.

"*Stupid stop!*" Mr. Dillinger called from the front of the bus.

"STUUU–PIDDD STOP!"

All around Travis there was stirring and cheering and even a bit of applause. They'd been waiting for this moment. A trip wasn't a hockey trip unless Mr. Dillinger pulled off for one of his famous "Stupid Stops."

Mr. Dillinger, his bald spot bouncing, hauled on the steering wheel and the bus turned sharply into an exit for something called "South of the Border" – a huge restaurant and shopping stop on Interstate 95.

Mr. Dillinger stood at the door as they got off the bus. He had a huge roll of American money in his hands.

"You know what a *per diem* is?" he asked as the first Owl – Nish, naturally – stumbled down the steps and out into the warm air and surprising sun of the parking lot.

"Huh?"

Mr. Dillinger was enjoying himself. "In the NHL," he announced grandly as the rest of the team emerged, blinking in the bright light, "every player gets so much money each day – that's what *per diem* means, Nish, *each day* – when they're on the road. They can do what they wish with the cash. Whatever they want."

"How much?" Nish wanted to know.

Mr. Dillinger scowled at him, half kidding. "Fifty-five dollars," he said.

"*Allll-righhhtttt!*" Nish said, high-fiving Data, who was standing beside him.

4

"You're not in the NHL yet, son – but there's a five-dollar bill here for every player who's made the Screech Owls."

"*Allll-righhhtttt!*" several of the Owls shouted at once.

They lined up and Mr. Dillinger, making a great show of it all, peeled off a bill for each player in turn.

"We can do anything we want with this – right?" Travis said, as he reached for the bill Mr. Dillinger was holding toward him.

"No, you cannot," Mr. Dillinger said, looking shocked. "You do anything sensible with it – you *save* it, for example, or *put it in a bank*, or fail to spend it absolutely foolishly all at once – and we will send you home for being too *responsible* and *mature* to be a member of the Screech Owls hockey club.

"Now get in there and throw it away – on something *stupid*!"

It took Nish about thirty seconds to find the joke centre. He was determined to follow the instructions to the letter. Mr. Dillinger wanted *stupid*, Nish was going to *be stupid*.

He talked Data into spending money on some hot gum. He talked Wilson into buying something called Play Sick, which looked, sort of, as if someone had thrown up and the mess had instantly turned to rubber. But Nish wasn't satisfied; he went off in search of more useless stuff, leaving Data and Wilson to fork out their five dollars for things they would never have purchased if Nish had left them alone.

Travis stood looking at a joke display. A hand buzzer. A letter that snapped like a mousetrap when you pulled it out of the envelope. A Chinese finger-trap. A card trick. He didn't think there was anything he wanted.

Suddenly Nish was at his side, hissing, *"Gimme your five bucks!"*

"What?"

"I need your stupid money, stupid."

"What for?"

Nish just looked at Travis, shaking his head. *"C'mere!"*

With one hand holding Travis's sleeve, Nish led his friend down an aisle toward a shelf at the back, where he reached up and plucked down something that didn't look the least bit interesting.

"You want to buy a pair of *glasses*?" Travis asked. What was wrong with Nish? This was hardly stupid.

"They're not just *glasses*," Nish hissed, holding them out like they were made of diamonds. "They're *X-ray glasses*!"

"What?"

"X-ray. You know, see right through things. See right through things like bathing suits. You get what I mean?"

"You're sick."

"I'm not sick – I'm short five bucks. *Are you in?*"

"You can't be serious."

"Dead serious. Now gimme your fiver!"

Travis reached in his pocket and took out his five-dollar bill. He knew better, but he handed it over anyway. Nish snatched it, giggling, and hurried off to the cash register.

What the heck, Travis told himself. Mr. Dillinger had said don't come back if you don't throw the money away on something absolutely useless and ridiculous.

And who better to show how it's done than Wayne Nishikawa, the King of the Stupid Stop?

2

NISH SPENT THE REST OF THE TRIP SOUTH hounding poor Simon. At the next washroom stop, he took the opportunity to help himself to a pocketful of paper towels. He waited until Simon dozed off to sleep, and then got busy. He carefully laid out several of the brown paper towels on the seat beside Simon. Then he took a bottle of water and sprinkled the towels and had Wilson pull out his rubber vomit and set it carefully on top of the dampened towels. He then took two more paper towels, soaked them, and laid them partially over the vomit so it appeared as if someone had tried to soak the disgusting mess up.

Then Nish really went to work.

He squirted the bottle of water directly into his face, took a paper towel, wet it, and placed it so it was partly sticking to his chin, partly lying over his shirt front. Then he turned toward Simon, made a horrible, sickly face, and began to moan.

"Ohhhhh . . . ohhhhhhhhh . . . ohhhhhhhhh!"

Simon shifted slightly in his seat, half awakened.

"Oooohhhhhhhhh! . . . Oooohhhhhhhhh! . . . Oooohhhhhhhhh!"

Everyone was watching now, and Nish twisted violently and moaned even louder.

"OOOOHHHHHHH! . . . OOOOHHHHHHH! . . . OOOOHHHHHHHHHH!"

Simon's eyes blinked open. They turned to Nish. They blinked again. Nish twisted and moaned.

"OOOOHHHHHHH! . . . OOOOHHHHHHH! . . . OOOOHHHHHHHHHH!"

Simon jumped. He looked down at the seat between them. He instantly went white.

"*Nish has thrown up!*" he shouted.

Wilson was instantly into the act. "*Oh my God!*" he said, as he looked over from the seat directly behind. "*Has he ever!*"

Simon reached out, frightened almost, and very carefully touched Nish.

"Nish. You okay?"

Nish opened his eyes and groaned. "Ohhhh!" He groaned again, louder. "OHHHHHHHH!"

Nish jerked toward poor Simon, his eyes rolling, his mouth opening as if he was going to throw up on him.

"*HHHELPPPP!*" Simon shouted, and he jumped so fast, so far, that he scrambled clean over the seat in front and landed on Data and Andy, who were crouched there giggling.

Nish was howling with laughter. With the wetted towel still stuck to his shirt, he was on his feet and squawking and flapping his arms like a chicken.

"*Wakkk-cluck-cluck-cluck-cluck-cluck!*"

It seemed everyone was laughing at Simon. Even Travis was kind of half-laughing – it was, after all, pretty funny. But it was also pretty cruel.

Sarah wasn't laughing at all. Nish didn't even notice her, though; he was laughing uproariously, his eyes closed and his mouth wide open.

Sarah reached down and snatched the rubber vomit off the seat and stuffed as much of it into Nish's open mouth as she could – which was more than you might expect.

"*AAARGHHHHH!!*" sputtered Nish as he spat it out.

"*Nish gonna hurl?*" Sarah asked sweetly.

"*Yuck!*" Nish spat, wiping his mouth with one of the towels. "*Whatdya do that for, Sarah? Geez!*"

"A taste of your own medicine," Sarah said.

"We were just having a little laugh," said Nish, sounding like he was the one who'd been hurt.

"Fine," said Sarah, "we'll all remember to laugh the next time someone pulls a mean trick on you."

"*Get a life!*" Nish snapped.

"*Grow up!*" Sarah shot back.

The rest of the trip passed uneventfully. Nish sulked. Simon and Sarah played cards. Travis dozed off and on and stared out the bus window as summer came ever closer.

Nish had glanced over at Travis while Sarah was ripping into him. Travis knew that his friend was looking for support, any support, but he had felt powerless to say anything in Nish's defence. Yes, it had been pretty funny. Nish, after all, was a good actor – he really looked like he was going to hurl. But if he was going to play practical jokes, he needed to spread them around, otherwise he was just being mean, not funny. Nish had been picking on Simon since Simon had started coming out with the Owls.

Suddenly, Mr. Dillinger began honking the horn. Once, twice, a third time, long and loud.

"*State line!*" he shouted back. "*We just passed into Florida!*"

"*Yay!*" the bus cheered as one.

"*We're there!*" Data shouted.

"*I wanna meet Goofy!*" Nish shouted. He was bouncing back.

"*Look in a mirror!*" Sarah shouted in reply.

3

THERE WAS NO TIME TO VISIT DISNEY WORLD that first day in Florida. In fact, it was getting dark when they finally made it to Kissimmee, the town nearest Disney World. When Mr. Dillinger announced they had just crossed over the Florida state line, none of them realized they were still four hours away from their destination.

Mr. Dillinger and Mr. Cuthbertson had made the arrangements. The Sunshine State Campsite had set off a special area for the Screech Owls and the other families who were camping to save money, the Cuthbertsons in their Winnebago included. Muck and the assistant coaches decided where the tents would go up and who would sleep in each tent. Travis and Nish were together in the Lindsays' big old family tent, sharing with Lars, Data, Andy, and, much to Nish's surprise, Simon.

"Lindsay," Muck said as he read out the list, "you're also captain of the tent. You keep a sharp eye on Nishikawa, understand?"

Travis nodded. How could he avoid keeping an eye on someone who always had to be the centre of attention?

Soon they had set up the old tent, and as they pulled their gear inside and rolled out their air mattresses and sleeping bags, Travis filled his lungs with the lovely, slightly musty smell of summers gone by that rose from the canvas. Next to skating out onto a fresh sheet of ice, Travis loved camping. The smell of rain through canvas, the sound of wind in the trees, the wonder of the life that was in every stream and pool and shoreline his family encountered on their annual summer camping trip.

"*Snake!*" screamed Nish.

"*What?*" Travis shouted. "*Where?*"

"*There! Under Simon's bag!*"

The head of a large snake was just visible under Simon's blue air mattress.

"*Lemme outta here!*" Nish screamed, scrambling for the exit.

Travis instinctively backed away as well. Weren't there poisonous snakes in Florida? Could it be a viper? A rattler?

Simon froze. He had been rolling out his sleeping bag, but now he stood absolutely motionless. Maybe it was a copperhead, thought Travis, his heart pumping fast. Andy was edging along the far side of the tent toward the door. He looked terrified. Lars was already outside.

Travis looked again at the snake. It wasn't moving. It wasn't even flicking its tongue, which Travis knew all snakes did in order to check their surroundings. Impulsively, he reached out and grabbed the snake and threw it, in one motion, out of the tent.

"*Rubber!*" he announced.

He could hear Nish outside, leading the laughter: "*Wakkk-cluck-cluck-cluck-cluck-cluck!*"

Nish was flapping his arms and walking around like a huge chicken, and Andy and Data were tossing the wiggling snake back and forth. It must have been what Andy's five dollars had gone toward at the Stupid Stop.

"Very funny!" Travis said as he came out of the tent.

"I thought so," Nish said defiantly.

Travis shook his head. Nish could be the nicest guy in the world one minute, the biggest jerk the next. He never seemed to know when to let up until he had gone too far.

"No more picking on Simon, okay?" Travis said.

Nish saluted. "*Yes, sirrrr! Mr. Lindsay!*"

Travis felt the morning sun, already hot, as it burned through the thick canvas of the tent. The air felt heavy, stale, and he threw back the flap to breathe in the fresh air and take his first look at a Florida morning.

It was a beautiful day, the dew sparkling on the grass and the pine needles, the campsite already alive with activity. Mr. Cuthbertson was headed down the pathway toward the showers, shorts on over legs the colour of milk, and a towel, nearly as white, slung over his shoulder. Muck, in his old windbreaker despite the warmth of the day, was at the Coleman stove, boiling water for a cup of coffee. Muck caught sight of Travis staring out from the tent and winked. It was just a wink, but it was all Travis needed to know that the Owls' coach, who hadn't much wanted to come when the Florida trip was first suggested, was now quite content to be here.

"Is it time to get up?" a voice broke from behind.

Travis turned, his eyes adjusting to the darker interior of the tent. It was Simon, and he was blinking through red eyes.

"Are your eyes ever red!" Travis said.

"They are?" Simon said, rubbing fists into both of them. "Allergies, I guess."

Travis guessed not. Unless, of course, Simon was allergic to Nish's taunts.

"Up 'n' at 'em, Lindsay!" Muck called from over by the picnic table. "We're on the ice in an hour!"

4

THE FOLLOWING HOUR HAD PASSED QUICKER than winter had vanished on the way down, and now the Screech Owls were on the ice and everything about it felt wrong.

The Owls had reached their destination only the evening before the tournament was to begin, and so had no time to practise. They were about to play the Ann Arbor Wings, a peewee team from Michigan, but instead of skating out for a warm-up and firing a puck off the crossbar to get ready, Travis was preparing for the match by hanging on to one side of a bedsheet, with Nish holding on to the other. Had there been enough wind in the Lakeland Arena, they would have been *sailing*, not skating down the ice.

"Fog," Muck had announced the moment the Owls got off the school bus and headed into the old rink. When the hot, humid Florida air from outside hit the cold air inside the arena, the result was a thick cloud of fog. It was so bad that Jeremy Weathers, who was to start the first game in goal, couldn't see to centre ice, let alone all the way down to where the Wings' goaltender was busy preparing his crease.

The Zamboni driver came out with an armful of old sheets, handed them out, and Muck and the Ann Arbor coach organized the players to skate about in pairs with the sheets billowing between them, trying to break up the fog.

"We look like ghosts, not hockey players," grumbled Nish.

"It's working, though," Travis answered.

It was, too. As the players skated about, they began to create air currents. From one end of the ice to the other, Travis could see the fog moving in chunks, first sideways, then up, eventually melting away. Players came into view, vanished, and appeared again. Nish was right; they did look like ghosts.

Finally, the referee blew his whistle at centre ice. There were still some cloudy patches, but the players could now see from one end of the ice to the other. They dumped the sheets into the outstretched arms of the arena attendant, and the game was on. No warm-up. Travis didn't feel right at all.

Sarah's line was first out, with Travis on left wing and the speedy Dmitri Yakushev on right. Nish and Data were starting, as usual, on defence.

For a moment, Travis was able to study the Ann Arbor team. They were larger than the

Owls, and had beautiful green uniforms with a magnificent white wing on the chest. He checked the winger opposite him: Nike skates, the best money could buy.

Travis shivered, then remembered something Muck had once said to them: "The one thing in hockey you can't buy is skill." Muck hated to see a kid come out with a brand-new pair of gloves – "You may as well dip your hands in wet cement," he'd say – and told them all that top-of-the-line skates were a waste of money for players who were still growing. "What's it matter if you start the season with an extra pair of socks and end it in your bare feet?" he'd ask. "Bobby Orr never wore socks in his skates – and he was the best skater there ever was."

Still, Travis felt a bit embarrassed by his equipment. His skates were not only used – "one season only," the newspaper ad had claimed – but they still had the previous owner's number, 16, painted in white on the heel, whereas Travis's number was 7. He worried sometimes that other players might think the "C" for captain was left over from another player as well. He wasn't the best player on the Owls, after all – certainly not when Sarah was part of the team – and he was almost the smallest. Before Simon had come along, he *was* the smallest.

The puck dropped and, instantly, the cost of equipment meant nothing. Sarah did her trick of plucking the puck out of the air, and Dmitri picked it up and circled back, tapping off to Nish, who was already moving to the side to avoid the first check.

Travis knew the play. He knew Nish would be looking for him. He cut straight across centre ice, one skate on one side of the line, the other skate on the other side. That way, even if Nish shot from within the Owls' own zone, Travis would still be on-side.

Nish fired the puck at Travis's head. No problem; they'd talked about this play before, though this was the first time Nish had ever attempted it in a real game.

Travis caught the puck in his glove and dropped it straight down onto his stick. He was free on the right side, Dmitri's side, and Dmitri crossed over onto Travis's wing. Travis knew that Sarah would have curled and would be directly behind him as he crossed the blueline. He dropped the puck between his legs and "accidentally" bumped into the closest defenceman, taking him out of the play. Sarah wound up for a slapshot, causing the second Ann Arbor defenceman to flinch, standing up stiffly with one glove over his face, but instead she snapped a perfect pass to Dmitri, now on his off wing. Dmitri one-timed the shot high in behind the goaltender, who had made the mistake of heading out to take away the angle from Sarah.

Owls 1, Wings 0.

"They're still in a fog," Nish giggled when they went off on a line change.

He was right. And so, too, was Muck. You can buy fancy equipment, but you can't buy skill. And skill was winning handily against the Wings.

By the end of the period, the Owls were up 4–1 on Dmitri's goal, a long shot by Andy that bounced once before slipping past the goaltender, a Derek Dillinger tip-in, and a pretty goal by, of all people, Simon, as he skirted around the Wings' defence and flicked a quick backhand over the goaltender's shoulder.

Muck had nothing to say to the Owls during the brief break between periods. They were playing well, but, more to the point, the opposition wasn't very good. Muck always seemed to worry more about games like this than he did about close ones. He said lopsided contests encouraged bad habits. What he meant, of course, was that the easier it seemed out there, the more Nish liked to hang onto the puck.

Travis sat and caught his breath. He had never played in such humidity. It seemed like he was *drinking* air rather than inhaling it. The others always liked to joke that Travis never broke a sweat, but he was drenched.

"Let's go!" Muck said when he got the signal that the break was over. "And remember,

Nishikawa, one superstar rush and you're on the bench. Got it?"

"Got it," Nish answered in a choirboy voice.

The Ann Arbor Wings came out with a little more zip this time and scored a second goal before the Owls took charge. But once they were back in control, the Owls slowly, simply, began to wind the game down. Muck didn't like it when a team – the Owls or anyone else – ran up the score on an outmatched opposition.

Sarah, in particular, was great at what Muck called "ragging the puck." She could hold onto it for ever, circling back and back until it all but drove the other team crazy.

"I'm gonna try a between-the-leg-er," Nish said to Travis as they sat on the bench after another shift in which nothing happened.

All winter long Nish had been trying to score a goal like the one on the Mario Lemieux video-tape that had come out after the Pittsburgh Penguins star had retired from the game. The Owls all thought it was the greatest goal they'd ever seen: Lemieux coming in on net with a checker on him and getting an amazing shot away by putting his stick back between his own legs and snapping the puck over the poor goalie.

"Don't even think of it!" Travis warned.

But the next chance he got, Nish picked up a puck behind his own net and came up ice, weaving and bobbing, until he suddenly turned on the speed and split the Wings' defence. He broke through and came in on goal, Sarah hurrying to catch up. She banged her stick on the ice twice, the signal that she wanted the puck.

Nish, however, had other ideas. Letting the puck slide, he turned, stabbed his stick back between his short, chunky legs, and with a neat flick of his wrists managed to trip himself – all alone on a breakaway! Wayne Nishikawa's reach was not the same as Mario Lemieux's.

With the puck sliding harmlessly past the net, Nish, tumbling on one shoulder, flew straight into the boards, where his skates almost stuck in they hit so hard.

The whistle blew and everyone raced to see if he'd been hurt.

Nish lay on the ice, flat on his back, moaning.

"You all right, son?" the referee asked.

Nish opened his eyes, blinked twice. "You calling a penalty shot?" he asked in his choirboy's voice.

This time it was the referee's turn to blink.

"What for?"

"I got dumped on a clear breakaway, didn't I?"

Nish struggled dramatically to his feet. With the small crowd of fans applauding to show they were happy he wasn't hurt, he skated, stiffly and slowly, straight to the bench, where he walked to the very end and sat down, removing his helmet and dropping his gloves.

He wouldn't be getting another shift this game.

5

"YOU GOTTA COME SEE THIS!"

It was Nish, and he was foaming at the mouth. Whatever he'd seen had got him so excited he hadn't even finished brushing his teeth – he'd run straight to the tent, where Travis was just putting on his sandals to start the day.

"*Where the heck are my glasses?*"

"They're on top of your head, dummy," Travis informed him.

Nish ripped his wraparound sunglasses off and tossed them into his sleeping bag.

"*Not these ones – the X-rays!*"

Nish was thrashing about the tent like a bear in a garbage dump, turning bags upside down, rummaging through everything he came across – whether or not it was his.

He emerged from his own corner triumphant. "*Here they are!*" he shouted, holding them up. "*Let's go!*"

"Let's go *where*?"

"Just follow me!"

Travis followed Nish out of the tent and quickly down along the trail leading to the shower and laundry facilities. Nish was breathing heavily as he ran, the sweat already blackening his T-shirt. He hurried ahead, then left the trail abruptly, aiming for a thick bush almost directly in front of the shower building.

When Travis caught up, Nish was already trying to put the cheap X-ray glasses on, but Nish was so sweaty they kept slipping off.

"What are we doing here?" Travis whispered.

"You'll see."

People were coming and going. Travis looked at men carrying shaving kits and women with towels wrapped around their heads to dry their hair – but he could see nothing unusual.

"*There!*" Nish hissed.

Travis didn't have to look twice. From out of the women's shower room came one of the most extraordinarily beautiful women Travis had ever seen. She was tall, like a model, and had wrapped a huge beach towel around herself for the walk back.

"*Damn!*" Nish cursed. His X-ray glasses had slipped right off his sweaty nose and disappeared into the thick brush.

While Nish fumbled for his glasses, Travis watched the woman walk away.

She seemed a little frightened, thought Travis. Not of Nish, who was thrashing around in the bush, but of something.

At the end of the path, two men were waiting for her. They both wore dark sunglasses. One, with his head shaved, wore army-style camouflage pants. The other, his dark hair tied back in a ponytail, wore a Chicago Bulls basketball jersey. They didn't look much like campers.

The man with the ponytail caught the woman by the arm as she passed and hurried her along the path in the opposite direction. The man with the shaved head waited, watching, as if checking to make sure no one was following.

"*Got 'em!*" Nish announced, emerging from his search. There was dirt on his face and all over his prized glasses. He looked absurd.

"*Where'd she go?*" he demanded.

Travis pointed past the guy with the shaved head. "Down that path. I don't think you want to follow, unless you want your stupid glasses broken."

"Whatdya mean?"

"I think that guy's a bodyguard or something."

Nish removed his glasses, blinking to clear away the sweat. A thought seemed to be registering.

"You think maybe she's a movie star or something?"

"In a *campsite*? I don't think so."

"Well, who is she then?"

"I have no idea."

6

"DON'T ANYBODY TELL HIM!" WHISPERED SARAH.
"Not a word – promise?"

She quickly went around to the rest of the
Screech Owls gathered in the shade of the trees
as they waited for the most popular ride at
Disney–MGM Studios: the Tower of Terror.

The Owls had risen early for their first full day
at Walt Disney World. They would do some of
the MGM Studios rides in the morning, then head
over to the Magic Kingdom, where they would
catch the parade down Main Street, U.S.A.,
before eating on the Boardwalk and waiting for
the fireworks display to close out the day.

The Twilight Zone Tower of Terror had been
a topic of conversation for much of the trip down
to Florida. Data, who had been to Disney World
only the year before, had talked about it endlessly.

"The elevator," he said, "drops thirteen floors
in less than two and a half seconds!"

There was just no doubt, from the moment
Mr. Dillinger had turned the full school bus onto
the entrance drive to Disney World, that the
Tower of Terror was a main attraction. Attached

to a huge billboard in the median were larger-than-life dummies suspended from a broken elevator, their faces filled with fright and their hair standing straight up on end.

"Looks like your hair in Sweden!" Lars had called back to Nish.

"Very funny!" Nish had protested, secretly delighted that everyone remembered the new look he'd tried out in Stockholm.

"He won't even go!" Sarah had shouted. "He's afraid of heights, remember?"

"*Am not!*"

"Oh?" Sarah had said. "And what, then, was all that fuss about when we were up the mountain at Lake Placid?"

Almost as if they'd planned it, several of the Owls had turned at once and, in exaggerated Nish voices, shouted out, "I'M GONNA HURL!"

"*No way!*"

"You won't go," Sarah said, sure of herself.

"A dollar?" Nish had challenged, his lower lip pushed out as he dared Sarah to bet on whether he'd go on the ride.

"You're on, Big Boy."

Even though they wouldn't be going on the Tower of Terror until later in the day, the ride – and the bet – were never far from their minds. The sounds, sometimes distant, sometimes close, of gear-wheels grinding, cables slipping, and riders screaming had followed the Owls around wherever they went – even all the way to Catastrophe Canyon. To half of the Screech Owls, the screams were a warning. To the others, an invitation. Travis wasn't quite sure how he heard it: he was half tantalized, half fearful.

The line-up for the big attraction was long. A sign that said they were forty-five minutes away from the actual ride. Fortunately, the wait would be out of the sun.

The line, twisting in a gentle curve rising toward the entrance, was shaded by shrubs and trees that were filled with birds. They could buy drinks and ice cream while they waited, and soon the big wait was forgotten as they talked about their day and moved ahead a few steps at a time. Several of the Owls tried to catch one of the speedy little lizards that darted up the walls and around the trunks of the trees. Data had his father's Polaroid camera with him, and desperately wanted a photograph of himself with one of the cute little lizards in his hand. But the lizards were too quick to be caught.

The two quietest Owls were Simon and Travis, each trying to calm his growing fears on his own. Nish had already predicted Simon would bail out before they got on the ride, walking around him with his arms flapping and doing that idiotic "*Wakkk-cluck-cluck-cluck-cluck-cluck!*" Travis dearly hoped it would be Nish, not Simon, who chickened out, and he planned to have the entire Screech Owls team do a "*Wakkk-cluck-cluck-cluck-cluck-cluck!*" around Nish when Sarah collected her dollar bet. That would serve him right.

Nish seemed to be gathering himself. The closer they moved toward the entrance, the quieter he became. He stood off to one side of the line, his eyes closed and his arms folded across his chest. He was in another world, dealing with his well-known fear of heights.

Nish didn't even notice when a brilliantly coloured bird landed on a branch directly over him and let go a sloppy white poop that landed directly on top of his head.

"*Scores!*" shouted Lars.

"*Shhhhhh!*" hissed Sarah, jumping directly in front of Nish and turning to the rest of the Owls, most of whom were pointing and laughing at Nish, who stood there with his eyes closed.

"*Don't anybody tell him!*" whispered Sarah. "*Not a word. Promise?*"

The Owls all stifled their giggles. Andy pointed silently to Data's camera, and Data got the message. With Andy and Derek's help, Data stood on the top of the concrete wall and aimed the Polaroid down at Nish's majestic new hair ornament. The camera flashed – Nish never even blinked – and Andy and Derek quickly helped Data back down onto the ground.

Incredibly, no one said anything as the line

continued to inch forward. Nish seemed only half awake, moving with the flow. A few tourists noticed, but each time they were stopped from saying anything by the Owls. Data pulled out the film and, when it was time, carefully peeled away the protective cover to reveal a perfect portrait of Nish's bird topping. The Owls managed to hand it around without breaking out into hysterical laughter. After everyone had seen it, Sarah took the photographic proof from Data and stuffed it carefully into the pouch she wore around her waist.

They reached the entrance without Nish catching on, and were directed into what looked like a seedy old, run-down, musty and dusty hotel. There were newspapers tossed on tables, with dates that read 1939 – long before even the parents of any of the Owls had been born! They passed through the lobby and into the library, the sense of dread building.

Once they were in the library, a bolt of lightning seemed to strike, bringing a dusty television to life with an introduction from an old show called "The Twilight Zone," which some of the kids seemed to know. A man with a deep voice made Travis shiver as he recounted the tale of the family that had disappeared forever when another bolt of lightning had struck the old hotel, causing the elevator they had been riding in to shoot out through the top of the building and far, far into outer space – all the way to "The Twilight Zone."

From the library they were ushered into the boiler room, where another snaking line led to the only elevator still working, the service elevator. Travis could almost smell the fear in the crowd. The screams from those actually on the ride were far, far louder now, the sounds of machinery grinding, then snapping, even more alarming. Travis's mouth felt dry; the palms of his hands were wet.

They had barely stepped into the boiler room when Simon broke. He just stood there, shaking for a moment, then suddenly turned on his heel and hurried back through the entrance.

Unfortunately, Nish noticed.

"*Wakkk-cluck-cluck-cluck-cluck-cluck!*" he chanted, with Andy joining in, both of them flapping their arms as Simon dashed through the door and away.

Their taunts made Travis all the more determined to stay – no matter how tough it got.

It was crowded in the boiler room: it seemed the walls were closing in. Travis had trouble swallowing. He knew from here they would be crammed into an elevator, and the idea of being trapped in that small space was as alarming as the thought of the thirteen-floor plunge.

The wait was growing worse. They moved by inches. The people seemed to pack in tighter and tighter. He was losing his ability to breathe. His heart was missing beats, trying to go faster than the heart muscles could pump.

There was a warning sign by the final steps leading up to the actual ride. Travis read the sign quickly: "*Those who experience anxiety in enclosed spaces should not ride.*"

Now he couldn't swallow at all. His shirt was sticking to his back. His heart was pounding. *He knew he had to get out!*

Travis looked around. No one was watching him; Nish and Andy were well ahead. Nish seemed to have somehow conquered his fear, or else he was just so determined to prove Sarah wrong that he had no choice but to follow through with it. Travis couldn't summon the same courage, false or not. He couldn't do it.

All eyes were on the entrance to the ride, all ears on the grinding gears and sliding cables and terrifying, hideous screams that came from above. Travis quickly checked the last sentence on the warning sign: "*Visitors who wish to change their minds may exit to the right.*"

For a moment he was undecided. He looked up toward the "service elevator," where the next trip was being loaded. Some were already screaming. A young woman lunged back towards the doorway, already in tears, but her boyfriend grabbed her and hauled her forward. Those waiting for the next ride laughed.

Travis couldn't take it. When he was sure no one was looking, he bolted for the safety exit. Through a doorway and up a quick, open elevator, and he was out into the Florida sunshine and could breathe again.

He had chickened out.

Travis was miserable. Even if he covered his ears, he could still hear the sounds of the Tower of Terror – the cables slipping, the gears grinding, the trapdoors breaking open, the rush of wind as the elevator plummeted again and again, and the endless, chilling screaming.

He waited around for the others by the exit, where he found a handy washroom. There was also a souvenir store, where they sold everything from T-shirts that bragged "I survived the Tower of Terror" to coffee mugs depicting the attraction. The store even had a booth where they sold photos that must have been taken at the very top of the tower, when the riders were at their most terrified. The billboard had been no exaggeration – their hair really was standing on end!

Travis watched as laughing, relieved riders came off the ride and entered the shop. He noticed Simon standing just outside the door.

Travis's first instinct was to call to Simon. His second was to keep quiet. He knew that everyone had seen Simon bail out, but he was fairly sure no one had seen him do it too. And since not all the Owls would fit into the same elevator ride, perhaps no one would ever realize he had chickened out. As long as Simon didn't notice him now, there was still a chance that Travis's secret would be his alone.

Feeling like a fool, like a traitor to his own team, he ducked behind a rack of souvenir coffee cups. Simon couldn't see him here, and his teammates might miss him as they came off the ride.

Travis heard the Owls coming even before he saw them. Loudest, of course, was Nish, and he was in full brag.

"*It was nothin', man! I shoulda bet twenty dollars!*"

They all rounded the corner at once, a laughing, pushing, shoving throng of kids in T-shirts they'd picked up everywhere, from Lake Placid, New York, to Malmö, Sweden. A few had Screech Owls caps on. Nish, of course, had another type of cap on. The bird plop was still there. It had survived the trip!

"*Hey!*" Nish shouted. "*Let's check out the pictures!*"

Travis could see Data wink at Lars. The Owls hurried to see the expression on Nish's face when he saw what was lying on top of his hair. Travis slipped unnoticed into the group.

"Great ride, eh, Trav?" Andy said as Travis edged up beside him.

"Yeah," Travis said. "Great."

"Which one were you on? I didn't see you."

"The other elevator."

Travis winced a bit. Technically, he wasn't lying. It obviously had been a great ride, and he *had* taken the other elevator. But not the next elevator on the ride.

"*Pay up!*" Nish was ordering Sarah up ahead. "I need some cash for the picture of me."

When Sarah held out the dollar Nish had won, he grabbed it and elbowed through to the front of the line.

"WHAT THE – !?" Nish shouted.

The man running the photo booth had just put up the photograph of the Owls' ride. Sarah's long hair was standing straight up, as was Lars's. Nish's hair was sitting flat, most of it trapped under a white mess.

"*This picture didn't come out right!*" Nish practically shouted at the man.

The man merely looked at the top of Nish's head and shrugged, smiling slightly.

"Looks pretty accurate to me," he said.

Nish slipped one hand up to his ear, then carefully onto his hair and up to the top of his head, where he found what he feared.

"*Who did this?*" he demanded, turning on the other Owls.

Willie, the trivia expert, answered: "I believe it was a cardinal."

The Owls all laughed, all except Nish. He yanked a Kleenex out of his pocket and began batting at his hair, disgusted. He looked around, spotted the washroom, and bolted for it.

"Quick!" Sarah said. "We've got to buy this for him. You know how Nish has to have a souvenir of everywhere he goes!"

They collected the money as fast as hands could reach into pockets and haul out change and small bills. Sarah made the purchase, and the man put the photograph into a bag for her to carry it in. The Owls then went outside to wait.

Simon was still out there, looking sheepish. No one said anything to him. Everyone knew what had happened, and Simon *knew* that everyone knew. No one, however, seemed to suspect that Travis had also bolted, not even Simon. Travis felt like a sneak, but he still couldn't let Simon know he wasn't alone.

When Nish finally came out, it looked like he had washed his hair – perhaps he had, leaning into the sink and scrubbing in that awful pink stuff that shoots out the soap tap. His hair was glistening and combed, with not a touch of white to be found anywhere. He did not look in the mood for teasing. He walked up to Sarah and stood directly in front of her, his lips moving furiously before he spoke.

"*Give me it!*" he demanded.

"Give you what?"

"The picture."

"What picture?"

"*The-picture-you-are-carrying-in-that-bag.*"

Sarah looked at her purchase as if she'd just noticed it for the first time.

"Oh," she said. "*This?*"

"*Give it to me!*"

"We were going to give it to you, Nish. It's a gift from all of us so you'll never forget your trip to Florida."

Nish grabbed the package as Sarah held it up to him, yanked out the photograph, and, without even looking at it, ripped it into little pieces. He then walked over to the nearest garbage can and dropped it in.

He turned, slapping his hands together. "There," he smiled sarcastically at Sarah. "Already forgotten."

Nish then turned on his heels and stomped off.

Sarah, far from beaten, merely smiled and waved at Nish behind his back. Then she patted her waist pouch, where Data's Polaroid still lay, well protected from Nish's chubby hands.

"Not entirely forgotten," she whispered, then patted the treasured pouch again.

7

THE SCREECH OWLS ARRIVED TOO EARLY FOR THE
parade down Main Street, U.S.A., so they killed
some time by poking around the stores. At the
Emporium, where Sarah and Data were lining up
to get their names stitched on the mouse ears
they had purchased, Travis thought he saw the
beautiful young woman from the campsite. He
told Nish.

"Geez," Nish said. "Why didn't I bring my
X-ray glasses?"

Travis shook his head: "They don't even work."

"You have to *believe* in them," answered Nish.

Travis just shook his head again. What was the
point in even trying to talk to Nish? How, Travis
wondered, did this lunatic ever become his best
friend?

Even without the help of his glasses, Nish
wanted to check her out. Travis had seen her in
the books section, buying a guide to the Magic
Kingdom, and they hurried over in order to catch
her before they left.

There was indeed a young woman there. She
was putting her purchase into a large pram she

was pushing, the baby shielded from the sun by a canopy.

"It's not her," said Nish, turning away.

Travis wasn't so sure. But he could have been mistaken. Perhaps the baby had just been sleeping back at the campsite and the man with the shaved head was her husband. Or the guy with the ponytail.

The Owls killed a bit more time by checking out some of the Fantasyland attractions – Mr. Toad's Wild Ride, Legend of the Lion King, It's a Small World – all of which they considered were for "little kids," not anyone who had ridden the Tower of Terror.

This, of course, only opened up more teasing opportunities for Nish. He tried to get Simon to take one of the rides, and for a while he and Andy and Wilson followed Simon around, taunting him in high, childlike voices: "*It's a small world, after all. It's a small world, after all. It's a small world, after all . . . It's a small, small world. . . .*"

Wilson looked very uncomfortable and quit after the first obnoxious verse. Andy quit after the second. Nish didn't know when to quit. He continued singing in a high-pitched voice while walking around behind Simon, until Simon looked as if he wished that he, like the star of Peter Pan's Flight a few steps down the street, could simply make a wish and fly away.

Travis waited until he had an opening. "Knock it off, Nish," he whispered.

"*Yes, sirrrr! Mr. Lindsay!*" Nish barked back. But at least he shut up and stopped singing.

"We better head off for the parade," Sarah said, checking her new Minnie Mouse wristwatch.

They were heading quickly back through Fantasyland and across Liberty Square, just opposite the Hall of Presidents, when Nish, at the head of the line, brought the Screech Owls to a sudden stop.

"*The Goof Man!*" he shouted.

Nish was pointing to the side of the building. The object of his attention, standing in the dark shade of the building, was concealed slightly by a parked maintenance truck.

"*It's Goofy!*" Data shouted, fumbling for his camera.

"*C'mon!*" Nish called back to them. "*I gotta have my picture taken with the Goof Man!*"

The Screech Owls turned like a swarm of bees, heading straight for the Hall of Presidents and the maintenance truck.

"*Hey!*" a uniformed maintenance worker shouted as they rounded the truck. "*This is a restricted work area. You kids can't come in here!*"

"We want to see Goofy!" Nish protested. "We just saw him here!"

The worker angrily checked his watch. "Parade's in fifteen minutes, kids. Catch him there."

Just then the side door to the hall opened and Goofy emerged: big toothy dog's grin, black floppy ears, eyelids half closed, red shirt, yellow vest, and black pants, white three-fingered gloves. Just like in the cartoon the Owls loved about Goofy trying to play hockey on a frozen pond.

"*Goofer!*" Nish shouted.

Goofy turned sharply to see who was calling, then began to move in the opposite direction. He has to get to the parade, Travis figured. He hasn't time for all the photographs and autographs the Screech Owls are going to demand.

Nish shouted after him, "*Goofy! Hey, wait up!*"

With Andy and Data behind him, Nish raced past the truck and brushed right by the out-stretched arm of the maintenance worker. Nish barrelled straight on down past the door Goofy had just come out of. He caught Goofy by the arm as he was about to slip away between two buildings.

"C'mon, Goof Man! All I want is a picture to prove I met you!"

Goofy turned, shaking Nish's hand off his arm. When he spoke, the muffled voice from inside the suit sounded irritated.

"There's a picture session at the end of the parade, son."

"We know that, Goof Man! But we'll never get through all the parents and strollers. Just a quick one, okay?"

Goofy shook his head impatiently, but Data already had his Polaroid out and Nish was posing for the camera as if he and Goofy were the greatest friends in the world. Nish had a big *hey-look-at-me!* grin on and had slipped an arm around Goofy's waist.

With no way out, Goofy gave up. He quickly threw an arm around Nish, posed, and Data took the shot.

"Only one!" Goofy said. "I gotta go!"

"No problem, Goof Man. We'll catch ya later." Nish didn't care. He had what he wanted.

Goofy hurried away between the Hall of Presidents and the Liberty Square Riverboat, and the Owls turned to continue toward Cinderella Castle for the parade. At the same time, the maintenance worker pulled away in his truck, veering sharply in front of the Owls. Travis got a glance at his face as he passed by. The worker looked furious. *How did he ever get hired here?* Travis wondered. Everyone else in Disney World was so friendly and helpful, but this guy had treated them as if they had no right to be here and had no right at all to be bothering a busy Disney executive like Mr. Goofy.

The Owls made it to Main Street, U.S.A. just as the parade was starting out, and they pushed as close to the front of the spectators' line as they could manage. It was wonderful, with marching bands and all the Disney songs and brilliantly coloured floats showing scenes from all the best-known Disney movies – *The Lion King, Aladdin, Beauty and the Beast, The Little Mermaid* – and bringing up the rear was a huge float with all the best-known cartoon characters: Mickey and Minnie, Pluto, Snow White, Donald Duck, Dumbo . . . and, of course, Goofy.

The Owls couldn't have been better placed. The parade stopped right in front of them for one of the "magic moments," when the cartoon characters from the final float came and danced with the children in the crowd and shook hands and posed for photographs. Travis shook Mickey Mouse's hand, feeling a little silly as he did so.

And Nish, of course, got a second chance with Goofy – who this time was in a much better mood. He posed for several photographs with Nish, then with Sarah and Jeremy and even Andy, who had been claiming he was far too old for this stuff but looked as pleased as Nish to stand arm-in-arm with Goofy while Data took their picture.

"*The Goof Man!*" Nish shouted, and Goofy turned and high-fived him.

Sarah just stood there, shaking her head in amazement.

"A true meeting of minds," she said. "It's almost enough to make you cry."

8

THE SCREECH OWLS AWOKE NEXT MORNING TO the sound of helicopters flying low over the campsite and then off over the swampy land to the south. They were so close that dust was still swirling on the campground paths when the boys emerged from their tent.

"Army choppers," Data announced.

"What're they doing?" asked Travis.

"Maybe somebody's lost in the swamp!" Data said, his imagination also swirling. "Maybe an alligator grabbed somebody last night!"

Travis didn't think so. Maybe there was an air-force base nearby. Maybe they were on manoeuvres. They probably hadn't been as close as it had seemed in the tent, the canvas shaking and the poles rattling as they passed directly overhead.

The boys saw Muck standing off to one side of their campsite, a big fist locked around a cup of coffee. He was staring after the helicopters.

"What was that all about?" Travis asked his coach.

"I have no idea," Muck said. "First there's searchlights passing through the campsite half the night, now these guys. I didn't sleep a wink."

This was no surprise to the boys. In a dozen long bus-rides – including this one to Florida – and a flight to Sweden and back, none of the Owls had ever seen Muck sound asleep. He might doze a bit, but sound asleep? Never.

"Must be someone lost," said Data, now more sure than ever.

"I guess," agreed Muck, sipping his coffee. He had things other than helicopters on his mind. "We're on at eleven against Boston. No morning swim – understand?"

"Yes, sir," Travis said.

Travis knew Muck was worried about the strong Boston entry in the Spring Break Tournament. Muck figured if they could only get by Boston, they stood a good chance of making it into the championship round.

"I want everybody on the bus by 10:00 a.m."

"I'll have them there," Travis answered. He was team captain. It was his job.

"We've got enough time!"

Nish was adamant. For breakfast Mr. Dillinger had prepared his great specialty – pancakes, sausages, hash brown potatoes, toast, and, on top

of the pancakes, a scoop of blueberry ice cream –
and after cleaning up there was still an hour to go
before they had to be on the bus with their
hockey equipment.

"No swimming, though!" Travis reminded
Nish.

"How much energy does it take to *look*?" Nish
almost shouted, shaking his head in disgust.

Travis gave in. "Okay," he said. "Let's get it
over with."

Nish gave one of his stupid yells – "*EEEEE-
AWWWW-KEEEE!*" – and bolted for the tent to
retrieve his ludicrous X-ray glasses. He and Andy
had come up with another dumb idea to spy
upon the gorgeous young woman staying at the
far end of the campground. They'd located her
tent the evening before, and today they'd go
down early, when everyone was beginning to stir
to start the day, and maybe catch her headed off to
the showers again.

"This time I won't drop my glasses!" Nish
promised.

They set off, with Nish well out in front and
Andy closest behind him. Travis, the least enthu-
siastic, brought up the rear, talking to Lars, who
wasn't much interested either. Lars also thought
the idea of X-ray glasses was about as silly and
immature and childish as anyone could get. But
he seemed to get a kick out of watching Nish be
immature and childish.

Simon was coming along as well. Nish had been about to go into his chicken act, but a sharp look from Travis had stopped him. Simon just seemed to want to be part of the gang.

The path leading out of the Owls' campsite crossed a dirt road, and they had to wait for a truck to pass. The truck had searchlights on both sides, and even though the lights weren't on, the boys felt like they were being examined. There were two men in the truck, both wearing dark sunglasses, both staring at them as the truck moved slowly by.

They hurried along the network of paths until they came to the far end of the campground. It was empty but for the campsite where the beautiful young woman was staying. There were more bugs there, and more undergrowth. It was a site most people would avoid unless they had no choice, Travis thought, but he supposed these people wanted to be away from everyone else.

"*Shhhhhhhh!*" Nish whispered, turning back and placing his finger to his lips.

The six Owls – Nish, Andy, Data, Lars, Simon, and Travis – all fell silent and ducked into the thick undergrowth by the path, where Nish led them, slowly, toward the campsite.

"*We're almost there!*" Nish whispered, holding up a hand to halt them.

He stopped, fumbled in his pocket, and removed the X-ray glasses. He put them on and pulled them tight to his nose and ears. This time, they wouldn't fall off at the crucial moment.

Nish took a step forward and fell flat on his face, his foot catching on a vine. He stifled a curse and yanked off the glasses. Then he stepped forward again, crouching low. He broke through the foliage – Travis could make out the campsite just over Nish's shoulder – and then repositioned his glasses. Travis could see Nish looking from one side to the other.

"*I can't see anything!*" he whispered back.

"*I told you they wouldn't work,*" Travis said.

Nish turned back, his eyes bulging behind the strange-looking glasses.

"*It's not the glasses, stupid. There's no one here!*"

Andy pushed through and checked the tents, without the help of X-ray glasses. He confirmed Nish's findings. "They're gone."

"Maybe they're at the showers," Wilson suggested.

"Naw," Andy said. "We would have passed them on the way."

"I'll bet they're at the beach," Nish said, his enthusiasm returning.

"We haven't time," Travis warned.

"Quit your whining," Nish snapped. "We've got time. Besides, these things were made for the beach – remember the package?"

"We can make it," said Andy.

"Let's do it!" added Data.

Travis looked at Lars, who simply shrugged to suggest they might as well get it over with.

With Nish and Andy leading the way, the boys began running for the beach. There was a back trail leading from this end of the campground to the lake. Perhaps this was why they had come to this out-of-the-way site, Travis thought. It had its own virtually private access to the beach.

The trail twisted and turned. They crossed a wooden bridge spanning a small creek, climbed over a fallen tree, and then came to a final bend in the path. The lake flickered blue through the opening.

Nish held up his hand to stop everyone.

"*They're here!*" he hissed.

Beyond the trees he could see two men on the beach pushing a rowboat out onto the water. The lovely young woman was also there, in a bathing suit. She was already in the water, holding onto the boat as they pushed it off the beach.

"*This way!*" Nish hissed, heading away from the trail toward a stand of trees near the sand.

For once, Travis agreed with Nish's tactics. It was a public beach, but somehow this morning it felt like the public was not welcome. Travis didn't know how, but these people gave the impression they did not want company, did not even want to be seen.

Nish held up his hand. "*Down!*"

The Owls all ducked down and scurried up to the thick stand of trees. Travis put an arm out and pushed away a branch. He could see very clearly now. The men were getting into the rowboat, which had been loaded with a large bundle of some kind. The woman, still standing in the water, began turning the boat with her hands, pushing it out into deeper water. The man with the shaved head, sitting in the middle, put oars into the oarlocks and began rowing, turning the boat some more. The man with the ponytail seemed to be tying rope around the bundle.

Now the woman was wading back through the water toward the shore.

"*They work!*"

The five other Owls turned at once toward Nish. He had his special X-ray glasses on, and he was leaning as far out from his cover as he dared, staring hard and grinning from ear to ear.

"*Fantastic!*" he said.

"*Lemme see!*" Andy almost shouted.

"*Me too!*" said Data.

"*And me!*" added Lars.

Travis turned, looking at Lars with surprise. Lars shrugged and looked sheepish. "I just want to see if they work," he explained. It didn't sound very convincing.

"Cost you a buck each," Nish announced.

"*What?*" they said as one.

"A buck a look," Nish said.

"No fair," complained Andy.

Nish made no reply. He simply stared, grinned, and kept congratulating himself. "*Beautiful . . . fantastic . . . I can't believe it . . .*"

Andy couldn't take it any more. "*All right! I'm in. C'mon, lemme see outta them!*"

"Who else?" Nish had to know first.

"Me," said Data.

"I guess me," added Lars.

"Me," said Simon in a quiet voice.

"Trav?" Nish asked.

Travis couldn't believe what he was hearing. "I already paid for half of them. Remember?"

"Oh, yeah," Nish said. "Sorry." He sounded more sorry for himself than for Travis, however.

"Lemme see," said Andy.

"Everybody's agreed then?" Nish said. "A dollar each."

Everyone except Travis nodded.

Nish smiled and took off the glasses, handing them first to Andy. Andy fumbled with them, dropped them, grabbed them up, cleaned them with his fingers, and pushed them on. He moved a branch away and stared out toward the young woman, who was still standing at the edge of the water, watching the progress of the rowboat.

"*Nothin'!*" Andy protested.

"They work fine for me," said Nish.

"My turn!" said Data.

52

Andy handed them over. Data put the glasses on and looked through the gap in the branches. He stared a long time before saying anything.

"I . . . *think* I see something," he said, finally.

Data slowly removed the glasses and gave them to Lars, who looked quickly.

"Nothing."

Lars handed the glasses to Travis, who knew even before he looked that he would see nothing. The lenses were ridged, so they gave a fuzzy-edged look to whatever you looked at, almost like a videotape on pause. Whatever the effect was, it wasn't X-ray.

"A rip-off," Travis pronounced. He handed the glasses to Simon, who didn't even bother trying them on.

Nish was still smiling. "I can't help it if they don't work for you. They worked fine for me. And Data."

Data didn't know how to respond. "I . . . guess," he said.

Travis looked back toward the water.

"*Look!*" he said.

"*We have been!*" said Andy.

"*No! In the boat!*"

The X-ray glasses and the beautiful young woman were forgotten as the six boys turned their attention to the rowboat, now well out on the water. The rower was standing up, as if keeping watch, and the man with the ponytail was attaching something to the tied-up bundle. The two men then pulled at the bundle and moved it to one side of the rowboat.

With an enormous effort, the men lifted the bundle, and Travis now saw that attached to it were two heavy concrete blocks. They steadied it on the gunwale for a moment, and then pushed it over. It splashed heavily and sank. The shift of weight caused the rowboat to rock so violently that the man with the ponytail fell back heavily. But the boat didn't tip over completely. The one with the shaved head quickly began rowing back to shore, where the woman waded out into the water once again to catch the boat and haul it up onto the sand so they could jump out.

"What do you think they dumped?" Andy asked.

"*A body?*" Data suggested.

Data – the most naive member of the Screech Owls – had the wildest imagination and came up with the silliest, most ridiculous statements.

But this time no one laughed. And no one had a better idea.

"We've got a bus to catch," Travis said.

The others seemed relieved to be brought back to reality.

"Let's go before they see us," said Nish.

He turned, took one look at the X-ray glasses in his hand, and tossed them into the bush. "What a waste," he said.

9

THE X-RAY ESCAPADE WAS THE TALK OF THE Screech Owls' dressing room as the team prepared to meet the powerful Boston Mini-Bruins. Some of the Owls laughed so hard they had tears in their eyes. Nish, of course, was convinced his tricking the others to pay a dollar each for a look erased the trick the joke store had played on him when he bought the glasses.

"No way anyone's going to make a fool out of Wayne Nishikawa," he announced as he began lacing up his skates.

"Is that right?" Sarah said, fumbling in the side pocket of her equipment bag.

"That is correct," Nish grandly announced.

Sarah pulled out the Polaroid snapshot Data had taken in the line-up for the Tower of Terror.

"What's *this*, then?" she asked no one in particular.

Nish looked up from tightening his left skate. His jaw dropped as he realized what he was looking at: a glorious photograph of the bird poop he had worn on the ride.

"*Where'd you get that?*" he demanded, the smile gone from his gaping mouth.

"Oh," teased Sarah, "let's just say a little birdie gave it to me."

"*You better hand that over!*" Nish said, standing up and falling at the same time, as his untied skates gave way.

Everyone in the dressing room again started howling with laughter. Nish scrambled back to his feet and began advancing across the room toward Sarah, who was quickly stuffing the photograph away.

"You're the big deal-maker," she said. "I'll make a deal with you, okay?"

"I'm not paying anything for that."

"No money," she said. "You take us to the championship, the evidence is yours to destroy."

Nish stopped halfway. He mulled it over a moment, then stared fiercely at Sarah. She had him; Nish couldn't resist a challenge.

"Agreed," he said.

Too bad they didn't have a few more embarrassing pictures of Nish, Travis thought halfway through the opening period.

The Boston Mini-Bruins had been a force. They had worried the Owls during the warm-up – no fog this time – with their size and shots, and

Travis had worried himself when he failed to hit the crossbar on any of his pregame shots.

The Mini-Bruins had taken an early two-goal lead, scoring first on a fluke breakaway that Jesse Highboy gave them when he tried a drop pass, and then on a point shot that went in between Jenny Staples' pads.

Muck had not been amused. He had warned them about the good teams from the Boston area. He had reminded them that many of the best players in the National Hockey League – Brian Leetch, for instance – were coming out of programs similar to that of the Mini-Bruins. "You'll probably be playing against some future NHLers," Muck had said.

And yet, if someone had walked into the Lakeland arena this hot March morning and been asked to point out the two peewee hockey players most likely to reach the NHL, they would have pointed to the Owls' top centre, Sarah Cuthbertson, and the big kid on defence, Wayne Nishikawa. Sarah's deal with Nish was working wonders. He was playing a magnificent game – blocking shots, completing long breakaway passes to Dmitri and Travis, playing the point perfectly, and carrying the puck, for once, at exactly the right time.

How to figure out Nish? To Travis, Nish was his best friend as well as the silliest kid he knew. He was a lazy hockey player one game, the hardest worker the next. This, fortunately, was one of those good times for Nish. He got the Owls back into the game on a brilliant move when he jumped up unexpectedly into the play. Sarah had taken the puck up ice and had curled off toward the right corner. Travis knew this was his signal to rush the net, and he raced in, fully expecting her pass. Instead, Sarah threw a saucer pass out into what seemed like nowhere. The puck flew lightly through the air, over the outstretched stick of her checker, and landed flat, perfectly, in open ice, where Nish, racing up past the Mini-Bruins' backcheckers, gobbled it up on his stick, deked once, and, using a surprised defenceman as a screen, roofed a hard shot the goaltender never even saw. Two minutes later, Nish fed Sarah a perfect breakaway pass that tied the game at two goals apiece.

How, Travis wondered, could Sarah and Nish seem such a natural mix on the ice and so different off the ice? When they weren't playing hockey, they were often at each other's throats, Nish baiting Sarah with his big mouth, Sarah refusing to allow him to get away with any of his nonsense. But watching them play this game, watching the way Nish jumped into Sarah's out-stretched arms after she had tied the game, Travis had to wonder if, in fact, Sarah and Nish were actually quite fond of each other.

The game remained tied right into the final minutes, Jenny Staples brilliant in the Owls' goal, the Mini-Bruins' goaltender spectacular in his end, stopping first Dmitri and then Travis on clear breakaways.

With less than a minute to go, Nish broke out of his own end and hit Dmitri with a hard, accurate pass as Dmitri cut across centre, Travis criss-crossing with him so they could change wings.

Travis loved this play. There was nothing he liked better than coming in on his off-wing, a left-hand shot on the right side, perfect for one-timers into the corner, where he turned, looking for a passing play. He saw Travis and fired the puck across, Travis one-timing it perfectly off the crossbar!

A Mini-Bruins defenceman knocked the puck down, turned, and fired it high to get it out of the Mini-Bruins' end. Travis turned fast, just in time to see Nish floating through the air like a basketball player about to dunk a ball, only Nish had his glove held high and had somehow snared the puck just before it made it across the blueline. The linesman signalled the play was on-side.

Nish dropped the puck even before his own skates touched the ice again. The defenceman who had shot the puck was down to block it, sliding on his side toward Nish.

Nish poked the puck and hopped again, this time right over the sliding defender, the puck squeezing through under his knees, the only space large enough.

Nish was in alone.

The Mini-Bruins' goaltender charged to cut off the angle. Nish deked once and sent a perfect backhand to Travis, who had an unexpected second chance – except this time the net was empty. He made no mistake, the puck bulging the twine in the centre of the net.

The Owls had won!

"I'll take my picture now," Nish announced after the cheering and back-slapping and high-fiving had died down in the Owls' dressing room. Even Muck had come to shake Nish's hand, while shaking his own head at the same time. Travis figured Muck was as baffled as he was by Nish's erratic bursts of brilliance.

"This just gets us *into* the championship game," Sarah said. "You still have to win it."

"Aw, come on!"

"That was the deal, okay?" Sarah said.

"No fair!" Nish said, slamming his gloves and helmet into his equipment bag. He slumped in his seat, exhausted.

Sarah looked up from her skates, and smiled. "Nice game, though," she said.

10

AFTER THE WIN AGAINST BOSTON, THE SCHOOL bus headed back to the campground. Mr. Dillinger drove slowly, with the windows down for fresh air and Derek handing out cold bottles of Gatorade from a case his father had purchased and put on ice for just this moment. Several of the Owls fell asleep, the game, the warm air, and the rhythm of the rolling bus relaxing them until they could no longer keep their eyes open.

Everyone woke, however, when Mr. Dillinger turned off the turnpike and suddenly braked hard, coming to a stop behind a string of cars. Up ahead, they could see a police roadblock.

There were patrol cars everywhere, several with their lights flashing, and the police and several husky men in suits were stopping the traffic in both directions.

"What's up?" Mr. Dillinger called, as he finally rolled the big bus up to the checkpoint.

The two police said nothing. A man in a light-brown suit – and with a wire running up from under his coat collar to an ear plug in his right ear – answered for them.

"FBI," he said.

Mr. Dillinger nodded, smiling, and waited for more information, but he got none. The police walked the length of the bus, staring up into the windows, and then signalled back that all was okay. Another police officer waved Mr. Dillinger through. The man with the ear plug said nothing.

"What did he say?" Jenny called from where she was sitting with Sarah.

"Federal Bureau of Investigation," Data called back impatiently, as if she should have known.

"What're they looking for?" Wilson asked.

"Drugs maybe," Data answered knowingly. "Murderers, smugglers, kidnappers, terrorists, extraterrestrial visitors – take your pick."

Once back at the campsite, the roadblock was all anyone could talk about. A man who'd had his trunk searched said the police had a clipboard with photographs of criminals on it. Another man said it was simply a precautionary sweep of the area before the President of the United States and his family visited Disney World the following week. A woman with her hair up in curlers said she knew for a fact that there were "illegal aliens" in the area.

"*Aliens?*" said Lars. "Like in the movie?"

Data happily corrected him. "'Illegal aliens' means people who shouldn't be in the country – not monsters."

"Oh," said Lars, a bit embarrassed.

But clearly, no one really knew the reason for the roadblock. Perhaps it was connected with the helicopters and the trucks searching the campground. But what were they searching for? It had to be more than merely looking for people who had sneaked into the country. Probably, Travis figured, the man who said it was just a routine sweep of the area before the President's visit had been right. Nothing to worry about.

The next morning the Screech Owls were headed back to Disney World, this time to line up for the popular Space Mountain ride at Tomorrowland and then, later, to take in some of the more athletic attractions like Blizzard Beach, where they would all change into their bathing suits and spend the afternoon flying down the greatest water slides in the world.

When Travis rolled out of his sleeping bag, Data was already up, sitting at the picnic table outside the tent and staring hard at some photographs he had laid out carefully in front of him.

"Have a look here, Travis," Data said, when he turned to see who was coming out through the tent flap.

Travis, blinking in the morning sun, rubbed his eyes as he walked over to the picnic table. All the photographs, he noticed, were of Goofy, several showing Goofy and Nish together.

"Which one's Goofy?" Travis asked, trying to make a joke.

Data didn't respond. He picked out two of the photos.

"Take a look at these two shots and tell me if anything's different."

Travis took the two Polaroid photos and examined them. One showed Nish, with his left arm around Goofy, grinning from ear to ear at the camera. The other showed him on Goofy's other side, again grinning from ear to ear.

"Taken from different sides?" Travis suggested. "I don't know – what?"

"Take a close look at Goofy's clothes."

Travis did as he was told. In the first photo, Goofy was wearing a yellow vest; in the second, the vest was orange.

"Goofy changed his clothes?" Travis suggested.

"He wouldn't have. He was racing off to catch the parade, remember, when this picture was taken." Data tapped a fingernail on the photo of Nish and Goofy at the Hall of Presidents.

"Maybe it's just the camera," Travis suggested. "Yellow, orange – they're practically the same. Maybe it's just the lighting. My camera does that all the time."

"Not this one," Data argued. "It doesn't mess up colour."

"Then there are two Goofys," said Travis. "Disney World's a huge place, you know."

"Maybe," said Data, looking unconvinced.

The line-up for Space Mountain was only thirty minutes long, and sooner than they expected the first of the Owls were being moved into little six-passenger rockets and heading off into the universe, shooting stars and meteors included.

The cutoff for loading one of the rockets came right in front of where Travis stood beside Simon. An attendant, holding out an arm, said, "Sorry, boys, next one," and for a moment the two Owls were alone with their thoughts.

"I'm just as glad," said Simon.

"So am I," said Travis.

Simon looked at Travis, wondering, afraid to ask.

Travis smiled, and all of a sudden he heard himself say, "I skipped out on the Tower of Terror, too. But no one saw me."

Simon's eyes went wide. "You did? Honest?"

"Honest. We'll do this one together. And if we can handle this, we'll do the Tower before we head home. Deal?"

Simon looked at him for a moment, blinking. He wet his lips nervously. "Deal," he said, and stuck out his hand. They shook just as the attendant waved his arm for the next six riders to board.

Less than three minutes later, their knees a bit shaky and their hearts still pounding, the two Owls stepped off the Space Mountain rocket and high-fived each other.

To get to Blizzard Beach, the Owls first had to walk back through the Magic Kingdom. Travis again noticed a maintenance truck parked to one side of the Hall of Presidents.

The back doors were open, and a uniformed maintenance worker was rolling electric cable off a drum and cutting it.

The man looked up.

Travis recognized him: it was the same worker they had seen here yesterday, but this time he was without his work cap and Travis could see that his head was shaved. It was the man from the campground who had been rowing the boat!

"Look!" Travis said to Nish and Data. "That's the guy from the beach."

The worker turned quickly and headed into the side door, the cable dangling behind him.

"I think you're right," said Data.

"So he works here," said Nish matter-of-factly.

It didn't seem right to Travis. Why would a worker at Disney World be living in a campsite? He kept worrying about it as they rode the monorail to the main entrance. There was a place just inside the gates labelled "Information," and while the others checked out a souvenir store, he made his way across to the stand.

A man in a Disney World uniform turned and smiled at him. "What can I do for you, son?"

"I just have a question," Travis said in a small voice.

"Shoot."

"Would they have more than one Mickey Mouse here?"

The man chuckled. "There's only one Mickey Mouse, son."

"But I mean for the parades and everything. Would there be two Goofys? Two different people in Goofy costumes, I mean."

The man shook his head. "Not a chance, son. People who come here *believe*. You understand what I mean? What if a little kid saw two Goofys? You can't have two Santa Clauses together, now can you? Same goes for Mickey and Minnie and Goofy. As far as this place is concerned, they're *real* people. We couldn't have two of them any more than your parents could have two of you."

"I see," said Travis. "Thanks."

"No problem," the man said.

But it *was* a problem. And Travis didn't know what to do about it.

11

"THERE'S NO OTHER WAY," SAID DATA. "YOU'RE going to have to dive."

Travis felt his heart flutter like the wings of a hummingbird. His breath caught. He felt clammy with sweat. But he also knew he could not show his fear. He may have chickened out of the Tower of Terror, but he couldn't back out of this.

The six boys had held a meeting in their tent. Data – and, to a lesser extent, Nish – was also sure that the maintenance worker outside the Hall of Presidents and the man in the rowboat had been one and the same. Data had photographic evidence that there were two Goofys. And the man at Disney World had said there could *not* have been two Goofys – at least not officially.

Those things the boys all knew for themselves. What they didn't know, perhaps couldn't know, was what the roadblock was all about, why the FBI was checking car trunks, why there were helicopters flying low over the campsite, and why there had been security personnel driving around in trucks with big searchlights.

And what, they kept asking each other, had been thrown from the rowboat?

Data was convinced it was a body. "The FBI solves murder cases," he said with authority. "Probably it's both kidnap and murder."

"Drugs," said Nish. "That's what they were getting rid of. They'll stash them at the bottom of the lake and then dive down and get them again when the heat's off."

"I agree," said Andy. "Drugs."

Travis didn't know. All he *did* know was that they were on their own with their wild suspicions. If they went to Muck or the parents, everyone would say that they were imagining these things just because they'd heard someone say "FBI." The photographs made sense to the boys, but anyone else would just think it was different film or a change in light that had made Goofy look different. Only the kids knew the other things that counted: the suspicious attitude of the first Goofy, the angry maintenance worker, the incident with the rowboat – and no one wanted to tell Muck why they had been spying on the young woman and her two companions. So it was up to them to get to the bottom of it.

And getting to the bottom of it, in Travis's case, meant diving.

"You're the one with the equipment," Andy had said.

He was right. Hoping that they might get out to the Gulf Coast and perhaps see some ocean life around the beaches, Travis had thrown his snorkelling mask and flippers into his backpack and brought them along.

"It's shallow," Lars had added, offering some comfort. "It's not even a real lake. It's manmade – a pond, really."

Travis knew he had no choice. "Okay," he said. "Let's do it."

They got the rowboat out onto the water with no difficulty. The boys all had bathing suits on. They had a strong rope that Data had found in the back of the bus, and Travis had his Swiss Army knife with him, tucked into the pocket of his bathing suit. Andy would row. Lars had borrowed a diving mask from another kid in the camp and was going to hang over the bow, looking down into the water. Nish and Data would sit in the stern for balance.

"Four's enough," Nish said, looking at the water line. "Besides, there're only four life jackets here."

Simon was odd man out. Travis had his snorkelling gear and would be swimming. But Simon had neither gear nor a seat.

"I'm a good swimmer," Simon said. "I'll support Travis."

Travis was grateful for the company. Together, he and Simon pushed the boat out into deeper water and then held on to the stern, kicking while Andy rowed out to where they remembered the men dumping the mysterious bundle. Once they made it to the general area, Andy began rowing in slow circles while the two with masks stared down through the water.

Travis felt uneasy. The water was clear, but the bottom muddy, with weeds. They could see fish swimming, mainly minnows at all levels, but once in a while a darker, larger shadow near the bottom. Travis presumed they were bass. He knew they couldn't be sharks in a freshwater lake.

"*Th-glub-r-glub!*" Lars shouted, his face in the water, from the front of the boat.

No one understood what he said, but everyone knew what he meant. Andy jammed down hard on the oars, bringing the boat to a stop. Travis and Simon let go and swam to where Lars was leaning over the water, pointing.

Lars lifted his face out of the water and yanked off the mask. It left dark red lines around his eyes and nose.

"*I think I see it!*" he shouted.

The Owls in the boat all glanced over, nearly tipping themselves into the lake.

"*Watch it!*" shouted Nish.

"*I see it!*" called Data. "*We've found it!*"

Travis stared down. He, too, could see the dark bundle. It was deeper here, but less weedy. He could see sunlight dancing on the bottom as the little waves played on the surface of the lake.

He blew hard on his snorkel to clear it of water, then he dived.

He dived into instant silence. He felt excited, but also afraid. *What if there were alligators in the water?* No, there couldn't be – the beach was safe for swimming. But what about snapping turtles? Why couldn't the little lake just dry up the way his grandparents' lake always emptied in his dream?

Travis was afraid. He knew it – he admitted it to himself – but he couldn't let fear stop him.

He looked up. Simon had taken the mask from Lars and was floating on the surface, staring down. Simon raised a thumb in support, and Travis felt a little calmer.

His breath was running out. He circled over the object. It was wound up in a dark plastic tarpaulin and held together with bungee cords. Lying to one side, attached to the bundle with rope, were the concrete blocks weighing the object down. He wouldn't be able to lift it himself. They'd have to use the rope.

Travis swam back up, his lungs vacuuming in fresh air the instant he broke the surface. He grabbed onto the boat, caught his breath, and realized there were four faces hanging over the gunwale and one staring at him from the water, all waiting for him to speak.

"That's it!" he gasped. "Hand me the rope."

Andy fed one end of the rope over the side; the other end he tied around a seat. Travis grabbed the rope, took several deep breaths, and dived again.

This time he had to go all the way down. He kicked hard with his flippers and felt the pressure rise. His mask pushed hard against his face. He kicked even deeper. He had good breath and felt strong, but he knew he was shivering.

A large shadow flickered underneath him. Travis could feel his heart slam against his chest, the effect all the more alarming under the pressure of the water.

The shadow moved again, slipping away. *A largemouth bass.*

If Travis had been able, he would have gasped in relief. But he needed every last bit of breath. He kicked again and headed straight down through a long curling mass of weed until he reached the bundle.

He quickly tied the end of the rope around two of the bungee cords binding the object.

His breath was running short again. He opened up the Swiss Army knife and cut away the lines attached to the concrete blocks.

He reached up and tugged hard on the rope, the signal that it was now tied on.

Before kicking to the surface, his lungs almost ready to burst, he took a final look. His tug had loosened the tarpaulin, a corner of which wafted back and forth in the water.

As Travis watched, a hand floated out!

His heart thundered. He almost choked, but he kept his breath, turned his face upward, and began kicking toward the surface.

He was panicking. It was as if all the nightmares of a lifetime were chasing him. He felt the hand wrap around his ankle, clenching, holding – tugging – pulling him back.

Travis wanted to scream, but couldn't! He kicked hard.

Then, even more firmly, something caught his wrist!

He looked up. It was Simon, his eyes bulging behind Lars's mask. He must have seen the hand come free, too. But he had still swum toward Travis to help, his bare feet kicking fiercely to get him down deep. Simon yanked hard. Whatever it was that had hold of Travis's ankle slipped.

Travis glanced back. It was just the weed. His foot had caught in the weed.

The hand was still hanging free, seeming to wave at the two Owls as they kicked hard and burst through the surface.

"*It's a body!*" Travis shouted as he broke the surface and spat out the mouthpiece of his snorkel.

"*What?*" Nish shouted, disbelieving.

"*I saw a hand!*"

"*I saw it, too!*" shouted Simon. He was trying to scramble into the boat.

"*Careful!*" Andy yelled. "*You'll tip us!*"

"*I'm not pulling up any dead guy!*" Nish announced.

Lars, fortunately, was in control of himself. "Everybody just calm down," he said. "We came out here to do a job, and we're going to finish it.

"Travis and Simon – you guys swim around to the other side to stabilize the boat, okay? We'll do the lifting from this side."

Simon and Travis quickly swam to the rowboat's far side, reached up, and grabbed onto the gunwales. Andy began working the rope under the seat so they would have some support as they raised the body.

The four in the boat gave a mighty heave, but nothing gave. They tried again, and suddenly the boat rocked violently from side to side.

"*It's coming!*" shouted Andy.

"*I–I'm scared,*" Simon whispered to Travis. Travis could see he was trembling, even though the water was quite warm.

"So am I," Travis said. "We get through this, the Tower of Terror's nothing."

Simon smiled, but his teeth chattered hard.

"*Heave!*" Andy called.

Simon and Travis could hear the rope rubbing and straining on the far gunwale.

"*Heave!*" Andy called again.

They pulled and the boat rocked, but not so violently this time. The rope was groaning with the strain.

"*Heave!*" Andy called, and with an explosion of trapped air the tarp broke the surface.

Travis and Simon held on tight, both of them shaking badly now. Andy reached over and grabbed two of the bungee cords, Lars grabbed another, and with Nish and Data pulling on the rope, they lifted the object up out of the lake – the tarp making a huge sucking sound as it left the water – and into the boat.

"*I'm jumping ship!*" Data screamed.

"*Hang on!*" said Lars. "*Look at it!*"

Travis and Simon, still in the water, had no idea what was going on in the boat. They exchanged startled looks. All they could hear was Nish's response.

"*I don't believe it!*"

"*What is it?*" Simon called.

"Have a look," said Andy. His voice was calm, without fear.

The two boys, with Lars's help, pulled themselves up to look over the gunwale.

The first thing Travis saw was the hand: white, with three fat fingers.

Then the face: grinning, gap-toothed, eyes half open, big black ears.

Goofy!

12

"THE YELLOW VEST," SAID DATA.

There was no need to explain what he meant. Lying in the bottom of the boat like a drowned cartoon character was the Goofy costume from the first photograph – the one taken outside the Hall of Presidents when they had encountered the maintenance worker who also turned out to be the man in the rowboat.

The other man in the boat must have been the person inside this Goofy costume. It explained why the first Goofy had been so anxious to avoid the Screech Owls. It did not explain, however, what he had been up to at the Hall of Presidents.

"We better talk to Muck," Travis said.

"We'll have to take this back with us," said Andy.

"*L-L-Look there!*"

It was Nish, real fear in his voice. Travis looked up with everyone else and saw that Nish was pointing to the beach. The beautiful young woman was there in a bathing suit. She must have come down for a swim, but she had turned back and was running toward the path.

"*She saw us!*" said Nish.

"Where's she going?" Data asked.

"To get the others!" Travis said.

"Let's hurry!" warned Lars.

With Andy rowing strongly and Simon and Travis holding onto the rowboat's transom again and kicking as hard as they could, the boys raced to shore. Travis was trying to picture the layout of the camp. The quickest trail back to the Owls' campsite would take them right past the campsite of the Goofy impersonators – they couldn't chance that. But there was another, longer, trail that skirted the campsite and ended up by the showers, which were close to the Owls' site.

"*We'll go back by the shower trail!*" Travis shouted up into the rowboat.

"*Got you!*" Andy called back.

As soon as Travis's flippers touched the bottom, he stopped swimming and pushed. Simon did the same. Andy gave one final dig with the oars and the rowboat ground hard onto the beach. The boys scrambled to get out, Andy grabbing the Goofy head and Lars scooping up the body of the costume for the run back. Travis kicked off his flippers and grabbed them.

"*This way!*" Travis called.

With Travis leading the way, the Owls raced toward the head of the second trail.

"*Hey!*"

The shout came at them like a gunshot. It was a man's voice, deep and angry. None of them had to turn to see who it was. They began to run even faster.

"*Hey! You kids! Wait a minute!*"

Another man's voice, this one with fury in it.

"*Drop that if you know what's good for you!*" the first man yelled.

Travis could hear the men running. They were well behind the Owls, but they were fast and, unlike Travis anyway, weren't tired from all that diving and swimming.

The men were gaining, quickly.

Up ahead, Andy rounded a sharp turn in the trail, hit some mud, and slipped down on his side, the Goofy head spilling into the bush. He got up, scrambling and limping. Nish, empty-handed, reached out and scooped up the head. Lars was well in front with the rest of the Goofy outfit.

Travis's snorkelling equipment was slowing him down. He tossed the flippers and mask and ran as hard as he could. He could feel his chest tighten. He turned his head briefly – just enough to see how far back his pursuers were – and in an instant he knew they were going to catch him.

This was real terror, true terror – not the manufactured terror of a ride. He felt like he was going to burst into tears like a little child. What would they do to him? *Kill him?*

The trail widened. He was almost home, but he knew that he wouldn't make it; one of the men was now so close behind he could hear his breathing. He tried one final burst.

The trail curled around a large sycamore tree, the moss hanging down from the lowest branches like a curtain. Travis recognized the tree. Once beyond it, he would be able to see the showers. There was the smallest chance he'd make it, if he could just dig down a bit more and come up with yet one more burst of energy.

But he had nothing left. He was exhausted, beaten, defeated. The man had him. All he could do was make it to the tree and, perhaps, a few more feet along the trail, and hope that someone would see him being captured.

As he rounded the tree he sensed movement, a quick blur, to his right, then the sound of two heavy objects coming together hard.

"*OOOOFFF!*" came the sound from behind.

Travis turned just in time to see the maintenance worker flying through the air, turning a half somersault before crashing, flat on his back, into the low shrubs and mud to one side of the trail.

Standing between Travis and the fallen man, leaning over slightly with his hip stuck out, was Muck.

The second, smaller man was coming up fast and had seen what Muck had done to his partner.

He was tired, his eyes wide in surprise, and he all but ran into Muck as he rounded the tree.

Muck stood his ground, both fists clenched. The second man put his head down and lunged, blindly, to tackle Muck around the waist.

Muck pulled back his right fist, took aim, and with one punch sent the second man into the bushes on top of the first, who was flailing desperately in the mud, gasping for breath.

Travis turned back up the trail. Mr. Cuthbertson and Mr. Dillinger were running toward him. Right behind them was Lars, who had been well ahead of the pack in the race back to the Screech Owls' camp. He must have run into Muck first and sent him back to rescue Travis.

Travis's chest was killing him. He had no breath. He couldn't even stand. He slipped to his knees, choking and coughing. Muck came up to him, ruffled his wet hair with one big hand and put the other on his shoulder.

"Nearly had you, didn't they?" Muck said with a bit of a chuckle.

Travis tried to answer, but could say nothing. He gasped for air. He put a hand to his forehead and it slid right off. He was wet with sweat.

The man with the shaved head was rolling about on his back, trying to get up. He had got his breath back, but it was too late; Mr. Dillinger stood over him, waiting. Mr. Cuthbertson was watching the second man, who was out cold from Muck's single punch.

The trail was filling with people now. They were running from everywhere: the showers, campsites, other paths. A truck with two men in military uniforms was pulling up as close to the trail as it could come, lights flashing.

The other Owls were first to reach the group. Andy and Nish in the front, Simon and Data right behind them. The rest of the Owls – Sarah and Jesse in the lead – were just coming onto the far end of the path, running hard to see what all the commotion was about.

Sweat was pouring off Nish's face. But he was laughing.

"*Great check!*" he said to Muck.

Muck couldn't help himself: he grinned.

"You said the hip check was a lost art!" Nish said.

"It is," Muck answered.

"Yeah, but you also said there was no place in the game for fighting, didn't you?"

Nish grinned like he thought he had Muck. But he didn't.

"This isn't a game, son."

13

IT CERTAINLY WASN'T A GAME. THE TWO POLICE officers who had driven up in the truck pulled out their handguns and held them on the two men, while another searched and handcuffed them, then shoved them into the back of a police car that soon arrived on the scene.

Before long there were more authorities swarming over the campground. They found the young woman and handcuffed her, too, and took her away. Then they brought in a special crime-investigation unit to begin studying the campsite and, most importantly, the Goofy costume the boys had brought up from the bottom of the lake.

Late in the afternoon, a silver-haired man in a light-brown suit, calling himself Agent Morris, came to talk to them. He was most intrigued by Data's photographs of the two Goofys and asked if the FBI could have them for evidence.

"You'll probably receive a special citation for this, son," Agent Morris said. "Good work."

"*I'm* the one who got Goofy to pose for the picture," protested Nish.

"Mr. Ulmar," Agent Morris said in a voice of great authority, "is the one who noticed the discrepancies in the colour of vests, sir."

Nish swallowed hard. "Mr. Ulmar" instead of Data. "Sir" instead of Nish. This was not a person to joke with; but then, this was no laughing matter.

Agent Morris explained it this way. The Federal Bureau of Investigation had received an anonymous tip several weeks ago that an unknown terrorist group would be trying something around the time of the President's planned trip to Disney World. The trip had been no secret; most of America knew he would be going and that he would be taking his family. The FBI, however, had almost no other information to go on. They didn't know the day – whether it might be before, during, or after the visit – they didn't know what terrorist group was involved, and they didn't know how the attack would take place, if it took place at all.

"The only other tips we had was to watch the campgrounds and keep an eye out for suspects working in disguise," Agent Morris said. "We knew our sources were excellent, but the information was far from perfect. That's why we set up the surveillance you encountered."

The helicopters had been to scare off the terrorists, perhaps even to flush them out if they were holed up in any of the many campgrounds near Disney World. The road checks, particularly on cars leaving various campgrounds, had been to look for suspicious characters.

"But since we didn't know what disguises might be used," said Agent Morris, "the road checks were pretty useless. If you boys hadn't figured it out for us, we might never have caught these people."

The FBI agent paused, swallowing hard: "And God only knows what might have happened . . ."

Agent Morris was being a bit too kind to the Owls. They hadn't actually figured it out. But the discovery of the Goofy costume had provided the evidence the FBI had needed to lead them to the terrorists. The man with the ponytail had decided to co-operate with the authorities, Agent Morris told them, and slowly the details of their plot were being pieced together.

The information officer at Disney World had been right when he said they would never have a second Goofy on the site. The terrorists had been able to bring the costume onto the grounds by having the young woman pose as a mother pushing a pram with her baby inside screened off from the sun. She seemed so harmless that no one had wanted to disturb her sleeping child, and she had passed through the gates easily. The man with the ponytail had simply paid to enter as a tourist. They used a diaper-changing room to hand over the costume, and the man had slipped into it in a washroom stall.

As for the man with the shaved head who posed as a maintenance worker, he had made it onto the site with forged identification tags and a perfect replica of one of the special uniforms the various Disney workers wear. Since no workers' uniforms had been reported stolen, there was no one on the alert for a maintenance worker, and this guy had seemed to know what he was doing.

The maintenance worker was able to get into the electrical works of the Hall of Presidents, which the real President was scheduled to visit in order to listen to President Lincoln's famous Gettysburg Address. The terrorists did not know, however, the precise time this would take place – the twenty-minute show played throughout the day – so there was no point in merely planting a bomb with a timer. What the maintenance worker had done was smuggle in three small but powerful homing devices in his toolbox.

Since "Goofy" could pretty much come and go as he pleased in Disney World, his job was to plant the devices in strategic situations. One, of course, had been in the Hall of Presidents. Another had been along the parade route where the President and his family were to watch the daily parade of Disney characters. "Goofy" had planted this one in the bottom of the parade's final float, the float that would be carrying the real Goofy, Mickey and Minnie Mouse, and Donald Duck down Main Street, U.S.A., right past the living, breathing, unsuspecting President of the United States.

"These homing devices could be used for a missile attack," said Agent Morris. "Whether they planned actually to attack or to threaten we do not yet know – but the important thing is that they have been stopped."

He paused again. "If you hadn't stopped them – we might have had a national disaster on our hands."

Agent Morris looked around, smiling, then shook hands with each of the Owls in turn, then with Muck, who seemed a bit sheepish. Agent Morris said to him, almost privately, "Thanks for being there." Muck only nodded.

"What country are they from?" Data asked.

Agent Morris didn't quite follow. "Excuse me?"

"The terrorists – where are they from?"

Agent Morris blinked, his distaste obvious.

"They're Americans, son."

Mr. Cuthbertson, Mr. Dillinger, and Muck called the Owls and their parents to a team meeting.

They sat around a campfire and Mr. Dillinger handed out soft drinks. Then the three men sat on a makeshift bench by the fire and talked about what the team had just gone through.

"I just don't understand how they could be Americans," Data kept saying.

"Anybody can be a terrorist," said Mr. Cuthbertson. "It's happened in Canada. A bit before your time, but your parents will remember. All it takes to be a terrorist is to be willing to do whatever is required to advance your cause."

"It seems so stupid," said Data.

"To the rest of us, it does," said Mr. Cuthbertson. "But an American can hate his or her own government, just like a Canadian. There's a world of difference, however, between disliking a government and voting against it and despising that government and seeking to destroy it."

"But they would have killed innocent people," Sarah said.

"That's why they're called 'terrorists,'" said Mr. Dillinger. "They spread the worst kind of fear. When you never know where they're going to hit, or *who* they're going to hit, it's very difficult to protect yourself against them."

"That's why what you guys did was so important," said Mr. Cuthbertson. "You may have saved a great many lives."

Everyone paused while this sank in.

14

THE FOLLOWING MORNING, TWO REPRESENTA-
tives from Walt Disney World came to the campsite, thanked the Owls for what they had done,
and handed out courtesy passes to the entire
team. The Screech Owls would have one last day
at Disney World. And that night they would
travel to Tampa, to the magnificent Ice Palace,
where they would play in the championship
game of the Spring Break Tournament.

"*Go easy!*" Muck called to his players as they
scrambled off the school bus when they arrived,
running and screaming toward the entry gates.
"*Save something for tonight!*"

But his warnings went unheeded. And
judging by the big smile on Muck's face as he,
too, hurried along, his bad leg swinging stiffly, the
Owls' big coach was advising caution merely
because he knew it was expected of him.

"You on?" Travis said to Simon as he caught
up to the smallest Owl.

Simon neither turned his head nor smiled.
"I'm on," he said.

The two friends headed for the Disney-MGM Studio lot – where the Twilight Zone Tower of Terror was waiting.

They both had a point to prove.

Fear sometimes felt like a swarm of insects climbing over Travis's body. He and Simon were in the long, twisting line-up for the Tower of Terror, eating ice cream and laughing. It would have looked like he was relaxed, but inside Travis couldn't shake the sense of dread any more than he could brush off a cobweb into which he had just stumbled.

Simon turned, still licking his cone, and said with a smile, "I'm scared to death."

"I am, too," Travis admitted.

They passed into the lobby of the old hotel, and were soon in the boiler room, approaching the terrifying service elevator. Simon had already gone beyond the point where, last time, he had bailed out.

It was in the boiler room that Travis had jumped out of the line, the words "*Those who experience anxiety in enclosed spaces should not ride*" sending shivers up and down his back as if he had a million spiders crawling on his naked body. Travis tensed, his mind fighting to hold him back.

He felt a tug at his arm and turned, panicking.

It was Simon, smiling. He had taken firm hold of Travis's wrist, as he had when the weed wrapped around Travis's ankle.

"We're next," Simon said. "You okay?"

"Yeah, sure," Travis replied. He wondered if his voice betrayed him.

"I'm not," Simon admitted. "Stick close to me, okay?"

Travis did not understand how Simon could admit he was scared when he could not. But Simon clearly needed Travis, and he wasn't afraid to say so. Travis had to stay.

The doors to the service elevator were open, the bellhop urging them in with an outstretched arm and a wicked smile.

Travis stepped forward, hesitated, realized with surprise that Simon was holding onto his T-shirt, then quickly moved along so that Simon would not see his resolve was crumbling.

Travis was inside. Simon was being shown to his seat, and when he sat down, solid safety bars were lowered across the laps of the riders.

The only empty seat remaining was beside Simon, in the middle of the last row, dead centre and completely exposed. The safety bar didn't stretch all the way across. Instead, a huge seatbelt was folded over the cushion.

"Right there, son," said the bellhop to Travis. "Best seat in the house."

The others on the ride turned and laughed, welcoming a little comic relief from their rising anxiety. All eyes were now on Travis. Everyone was watching. He couldn't break down here.

"Th-th-thanks," said Travis. He started to put on his seatbelt, but his hands were shaking badly. The bellhop grabbed the two ends and fitted them together.

"There's nothing to it, son," he whispered before leaving. The bellhop knew. He probably knew *every* time someone had gone further than he or she intended and was trapped in the ride.

The moment the door closed, Travis felt as if his throat had also been slammed tight. He had no air. He was bursting. He twisted hard against the seatbelt, but the straps held him in. He felt if his body couldn't leave the seat, his heart would leave his body – ripping right through his rib cage.

He felt Simon's hand on his forearm. Simon's palm was soaking wet. He needed Travis.

Travis very deliberately began to suck in a breath. He took it slowly and carefully, and felt the air go deep. His heart settled, at least for the moment.

The elevator rose slowly, then stopped, and the doors opened onto an endless corridor. The family of hotel guests who had disappeared back in 1939 – the parents, a little girl – suddenly appeared as holograms, checking into their rooms, then vanishing into ghostly memory.

Travis felt Simon's fingernails dig into his forearm.

The doors closed, and up again went the elevator. It stopped and then slipped sideways out of the shaft and began moving across the hotel. They were surrounded by stars and blackness. It felt as if they were floating in outer space.

He had gone much too far! There was no last-minute exit here!

Again, Travis's breath refused to come. Again, he felt Simon holding on. Travis had to be brave. He was . . . *Captain.*

With a bump the elevator stopped rolling and began to rise. These were the sounds they had heard from outside, the sounds of cables working, cables snapping, that always preceded the terrifying screams from the riders.

"*Oh my God! Oh my God!*" a woman shouted from the front row. The other riders laughed, but as they did, Travis could hear their own anxiety.

Up, up, up rose the elevator, the cables creaking, the tension rising. The cables groaned, seemed to pause momentarily, and then, *snap*, the elevator plunged like a stone!

"*Heaven help us!*" screamed the woman in the front row. No one laughed this time.

Travis knew he too was screaming. He knew his mouth was open. He could feel his hair lifting in the downward rush. He knew, in that instant, he would give anything in the world to get out of that elevator. He would give up his collection of NHL cards, his posters of Mats Sundin and Paul Kariya and Doug Gilmour. He would give up being Captain, his chance at an NHL career. *Anything* to get out of there!

The elevator came to a sudden halt.

He was still alive!

He turned to Simon. His friend looked like he had just swallowed an alligator. His eyes were bulging, his cheeks puffed. Pure terror was written all over Simon's face, and yet the ride was only just beginning.

Again the cables creaked, again the elevator began to rise, only this time with gathering speed.

As the elevator rose faster and faster, it began to feel as out of control as a free-fall. It seemed as if it would crash through the roof and head off into outer space – just like in the Twilight Zone film they had seen.

Up and up, faster and faster still. Travis grabbed onto Simon, Simon onto Travis. People were screaming. The woman in the front row was screaming and praying. Then suddenly, in a flash, they were outside! The roof gave way, and the elevator, for the briefest moment, seemed to lunge out over the Studio lot!

An explosion of light blinded them! Was it just the sudden sun? Was it a camera flash?

"*OHHHHHH MY GODDDDDD!!!*" the

woman in the front row screeched. This was not for effect. She was terrified.

"*We're all gonna die!*" shouted a man.

"*Alllll Riggghhhhhtttttt!!!*" screamed another, excited voice.

Travis turned quickly in shock. *It was Simon who had screamed!* He was smiling from ear to ear!

The elevator was plunging. Down thirteen floors in less than three seconds. Travis had never felt such pressure against him – G-force, they called it. It pushed against his face, his arms, his back. It was more powerful than anything he had ever felt diving, more powerful than anything he had ever felt in an airplane. It was pure terror – a force so wild and uncontrollable he was completely helpless. Travis could not have moved even if he'd wanted to. He could not fight it. He had to go with it.

He was on this ride to the end.

"*Fantastic!*" Simon shouted as they left the elevator, their legs a bit rubbery and their eyes blinking fast, unaccustomed to the light.

Travis couldn't stop giggling. He had done it. He had mastered his fear and stayed to the end – not that he had much choice once the bellhop had strapped him in. But far more important than merely lasting, he had *enjoyed* it. There was something about the thrill of utter helplessness.

"*Great!*" he said.

Three times they had risen and plunged. On the third ride up, there was no longer terror in the riders' screams; on the third plunge, the screaming had become a celebration. Had it been put to a vote, they would have gone for a fourth, easily.

"I have to go to the washroom," said Simon.

"I'll wait in here for you," said Travis, heading into the souvenir shop.

Travis didn't think Simon knew about the photographs. He would buy him one for proof – proof, if he ever needed it again, that he hadn't been afraid.

The man at the photo booth was just putting up the photograph of their ride. Travis was amazed that his hair could stand so straight up, stunned that he could look so terrified and moments later be laughing about it. Simon, sitting beside him in the picture, looked like one of the dummies advertising the ride on the way into Disney World.

He quickly paid for the photograph and tucked it in under his shirt.

Simon was just coming out of the washroom when Travis got back. "Anything good?" he asked.

"Naw," Travis said. "Let's go."

15

ONCE AGAIN TRAVIS HAD TROUBLE CATCHING HIS
breath. Once again he felt clammy all over with
nervous sweat, his heart pounding out of control.
But there was nothing closed-in about this space.

They were in the Ice Palace, a huge hockey
rink that could hold more than twenty thousand
people. He could barely see to the rafters. Even
the Screech Owls' dressing room was bigger than
any he'd ever been in.

He looked up and saw hundreds of, if not
twenty thousand, fans. All the parents were there,
and all the relatives of the team they would be
playing.

Their championship game against the State
Selects – an all-star team made up of the very
best players from all over the state of Florida –
was even going to be broadcast. And in two lan-
guages – but not French and English, as would
happen back in Canada, but in English and
Spanish. The radio station that carried the
Florida Panthers' games in Spanish – the first
hockey games ever broadcast in that language –
had decided to come up to Tampa once the

Selects had made it to the final, and now half the kids on the Owls' team were shouting out, "*Se metio-ooooo!*" – the Spanish equivalent of, "*He shoots! He scores!*"

Muck had told the Owls to "save something" for tonight, and if they lacked anything in energy, they more than made up for it in enthusiasm. The size, the lights, the *professionalism* of the Ice Palace had them fired up. So, too, had the fans. Their own relatives were there, yes, but there was also a group from Disney World, and even Agent Morris and his family.

"This is a serious team," Muck had told them before the Owls came out onto the ice. "Hockey has taken off in Florida the past few years, so don't think you're up against a bunch of surfers and beach bums. They're a good, fast, big team, and they're very well coached. I should know: Deke Larose, their coach, played with me once. He knows his hockey."

Travis could tell during the warm-up that Muck had been right. The Selects were very well organized. The goaltender looked great and, obviously, had a great glove hand.

"Sarah's line starts," Muck had said just before the Owls left the big dressing room. "Jenny's our goalie tonight."

"*Let's go, Jenny!*" Sarah had yelled.

"*Jen-ny!*"

"*Jen-ny!*"

Not long after, Travis understood why Muck had named Jenny to start, and not Jeremy, who usually played the big games. They were all turned toward the Canadian flag for "O Canada," when the Selects' goaltender yanked off her helmet. The Selects also had a girl in net. Muck must have figured the challenge would inspire Jenny.

Sarah took the face-off – *and lost it!* Travis was shocked. Sarah rarely lost a face-off. But this one she lost clean, the big Selects' centre backhanding the puck to his left defenceman.

Dmitri moved quickly to check the defender, catching the youngster off guard with his extra-ordinary speed. Panicking, the defender tried to fire the puck back to his centre, but the puck bounced straight up ice into Dmitri's shin pads.

In an instant Dmitri was around the falling defenceman and racing in alone. Travis hurried in case there was a rebound, but he didn't expect one. He had seen Dmitri do this too many times. In hard, a shoulder fake, then onto the backhand and a high roofer to the short side.

Dmitri faked, pulled the puck onto his backhand, and, just as Travis had anticipated, rifled the puck high and hard into the open side of the net.

Only it never got there! A white glove flashed, and the puck disappeared! Dmitri curled away, looking back in surprise. The referee's whistle blew. The Selects' goaltender flipped the puck out and caught it again on the webbing of her glove, then presented it to the referee as casually as if he were at a garden party and she were serving little munchies on a platter.

"*Did you see that catch?*" Nish asked, when he and Travis came off at the end of the first shift.

"Great glove hand!" Travis agreed.

The Selects were indeed well coached. Unlike so many other all-star teams the Owls had played, this one truly was a *team*. There was no hot-dogging, no heroics, no end-to-end rushes. The players had a system, and each knew exactly where he or she fit into the system. They always sent one player in to forecheck, hoping to force a pass while the others clogged up the middle.

"*They're trapping us,*" Muck said behind the bench.

"I can't believe it," said Mr. Dillinger.

Wilson got caught circling his own net and tried a pass to Simon, standing up along the blue-line, but the waiting Selects forward pounced on it. Simon might have made a diving check, but chose instead to chase.

The Selects forward passed to his opposite winger in the corner, who then passed quickly to the centre driving in toward the slot. Simon, hurrying back, tried to play the puck, not the man, and the big centre merely stepped around him and drove a hard shot over Jenny's shoulder.

Selects 1, Owls 0.

"We gotta do something about that trap," Muck said, as he sent Sarah's line out again.

"Nishikawa – come back here."

Nish skated back to the bench and conferred with Muck. The referee blew his whistle to get the Owls moving, and Muck slapped Nish's back and sent him into the play.

Nish detoured past Travis as they lined up for the face-off.

"I get the puck," Nish whispered to him. "You head for centre ice."

Sarah won this draw. She pivoted with it, avoided one check, and then dropped it back to Nish, who skated hard for the back of the net, stopping in a spray with the puck and waiting while the Selects sent in their single forechecker.

Nish faked going to the far side and, immediately, the forechecker moved to force him tight, counting on another cross-ice pass that they could then intercept. But Nish dug in hard and turned the other way.

Travis was already breaking for centre ice. Nish rounded the net and lifted the puck so high it almost struck the clock, floating high and falling just beyond centre ice, where Travis, barely on side, picked it up and was in free.

He knew he had to keep it away from the goalie's glove hand. He came in, his mind spinning with far too many questions. Should he shoot? Deke? Backhand? Forehand? He looked up. No openings. He looked down, the puck beginning to skid off the blade of his stick. He lost it, regained it, and shot without looking.

Again the white blur! Again the puck vanished!

"You should have gone stick side," Nish said when they got back to the bench.

"Five hole," said Dmitri.

"Just rip it!" said Sarah.

Everybody had a suggestion; no one had an answer.

Then the Selects got a power play when Andy took a penalty for tripping, and a hard shot from the point went in off Nish's toe.

Selects 2, Owls 0.

"My fault," Andy said to Jenny when the Owls went to console her.

"I should have had it," Jenny said.

Travis looked hard at Jenny. At first he thought she was near tears, but then he realized she was just angry. Muck had offered her this challenge, and the Selects' goaltender was beating her.

The Owls barely held off the Selects for the remainder of the period. If it hadn't been for Sarah's checking and a great shot block by Andy, the Selects would have run away with the game. As it was, the Owls were barely hanging on.

Muck waited until they had caught their breath before he entered the dressing room. Nish, as usual, had his head down almost between his legs. Sarah and Travis were sagging, their backs against the lockers, their gloves and helmets off. Sweat was dripping freely from Sarah's face. Travis, too, was sweating heavily for once.

Muck was smiling. He didn't seem the slightest bit concerned.

"Jenny just forgot to turn on her equipment," he said. "Those guys aren't going to get another shot past her – guaranteed."

Jenny didn't look up. She hadn't even removed her mask. She just sat, staring straight ahead, ready to go on a moment's notice.

"Nishikawa," Muck said.

Nish looked up, expecting a blast.

"I like what I see out there. Let's see a bit more of it, though."

Nish looked down, the colour rising in his face.

"Higgins," Muck said, turning on big Andy, who'd played well apart from the penalty.

Andy looked up, waiting.

"I want to try something: you on a line with Simon and Jesse. I think you're due, Simon."

Simon looked bewildered. He hadn't played particularly well. He'd lost the puck that led to the Selects' first goal.

Muck walked out the door, leaving them to their thoughts.

"You should have had that guy," Nish said across the dressing room to Simon. "He was your check."

Simon twisted defensively: "Don't think I don't know that."

"You can't be afraid of the puck," Nish said in a quiet voice, but one that everyone heard.

"I'm not," Simon said.

"Prove it, then," Nish said.

"Cut it out," Sarah interrupted. "You're not in a position to ask for proof."

"What's that supposed to mean?" Nish demanded.

Sarah answered by pulling an envelope from the side pocket of her equipment bag. She opened the envelope and took out the Polaroid of Nish wearing his bird dropping.

"You're supposed to give me that!" Nish whined, angry at the sight of the reminder.

"We're down 2–0, Bird Poo," said Sarah.

Nish buried his head again in his knees. Simon starting tapping his stick on the ends of his skates.

Travis was captain. He knew he had to stay something.

"Don't forget we're a team," he said. "Don't forget what got us here."

"*Let's go!*" Dmitri shouted from the far side of the room.

"*Let's do it!*" shouted Jesse.

"*We're the Screech Owls!*" shouted Sarah.

"*Owls!*"

"*Owls!*"

"*Owls!*"

16

NISH WAS AGAIN A DRIVEN PLAYER IN THE second period. He blocked shots, cut off rushes, and twice tried the sneak pass over centre, but the first time the Selects were waiting on it and beat Dmitri to the puck.

The second time it worked. Andy stepped in front of one Selects defenceman, "accidentally" blocking his route, and little Simon squirted out of the pack to take the lead in the rush for the puck Nish had sent flying over centre.

"*Go, Simon!*" Sarah screamed from the bench.

Simon was so nervous he almost lost his footing as he picked up the wobbling puck. He came in over the blueline, wound up for a slap-shot, faked it, and moved to the far side of the net before sliding the puck in between the goal-tender's outstretched legs.

Selects 2, Owls 1.

"*Five hole!*" shouted Dmitri. "*Told you so!*"

The Owls' bench went wild. Even Muck and Mr. Dillinger high-fived each other.

Nish, hurrying up behind Simon, caught him in a bear hold as he stepped off the ice and almost twisted his helmet off.

Simon's goal gave the Owls new life. They played far better in the second period, not once letting the Selects trap them on a breakout play. Their opponents were getting frustrated, particularly with Sarah's close checking, which was keeping the Selects' big centre under control.

With less than a minute to go in the second, Data picked up a loose puck in the Owls' corner and clipped it off the boards to Travis, who saw Nish shooting up into the play. Nish took the puck and charged over centre, the backchecking Selects winger unable to stay with him.

Nish flipped the puck again. Not high toward the clock this time, but a gentle little flick that sent the puck between the two defencemen who were beginning to squeeze toward him. Both defence decided to play the man and went for Nish, but Nish jumped high, right between them. He was home free, until he lost his grip and fell.

Nish spun toward the corner, the puck still on his stick. Flat on his stomach, he managed to look up and see Sarah coming in along the near side. He swept the puck to her just before crashing into the boards, and Sarah fired a pass hard across the crease to Dmitri, who had the whole open side of the net to tap the puck into.

Selects 2, Owls 2.

When the second period was up, the Owls skated off to a huge ovation for their comeback. Even Agent Morris of the FBI was on his feet. And all the Disney people.

"Delay Nish for a bit," Sarah said to Travis.

Travis nodded. He waited at the boards, slapping each teammate as the player left the ice, and then grabbed Nish as he was coming off.

"Spanish radio wants to interview you," Travis told him.

Nish stopped dead in his tracks. "*I can't speak Spanish!*" he said.

"Doesn't matter – they'll translate."

"Where do I go?" Nish asked. He didn't seem surprised that they would want to interview him.

"You just wait here," Travis said. "They'll come down to you."

Travis hurried into the dressing room, giggling at his own trick. Sarah was already at work. She had taken the scissors Mr. Dillinger used to cut away tape and was chopping up the Polaroid of Nish into dozens of little pieces, which she then piled carefully on his locker seat.

"Is he coming?" she asked.

"He thinks he's about to be interviewed on Spanish radio," Travis said.

The rest of the Owls looked up, realized the trick that had been played, and roared with laughter.

The door banged open and Nish roared in, furious, throwing his stick and turning on Travis.

"*There was no one there to interview me!*"

Nish was beet-red, his face contorted with anger. Travis knew he'd have to do some fancy talking to save this one.

"I guess I got the periods wrong," Travis said. "They must have meant the end of the game. The guy didn't speak English that well."

Nish considered this to make great sense.

"Okay," he said. "But don't waste my time like that again."

Nish wandered over to his seat, dropping his gloves and helmet.

"*What's this?*" he asked.

He brushed away the pieces of the incriminating photograph. "Thank you, thank you, thank you," he said to no one in particular.

"You're playing great hockey," said a familiar voice from the back of the room.

It was Muck.

"Thank you," said Nish again. He thought Muck was speaking directly to him.

"All of you," said Muck. "I have nothing more to tell you."

And with that, Muck walked out of the dressing room, smiling.

17

WHETHER JENNY HAD "TURNED HER EQUIPMENT on" or not didn't matter. She was spectacular in the third period, on one occasion stopping the big centre on a clear breakaway.

But Jenny had some help. She got it from Nish (who seemed to block as many shots as she did), and she got it from Data (who kept clearing the puck) and Sarah (who backchecked with ferocious energy). At the other end, Travis and Dmitri kept up a solid forecheck, causing turnover after turnover. The brilliant glove hand of the Selects' goalie took away a sure goal from Andy, and an excellent poke check stopped Travis on what looked like an easy tap-in.

Regulation time came to an end with the teams still tied. Muck spoke to them before the five-minute overtime.

"They're starting to send in two forecheckers," said Muck. "I know Deke's style. He figures to panic our defence. Nishikawa?"

"Yes, sir."

"You like to carry the puck, don't you?"

"Sometimes."

"If you get a chance, go for it. We cut off their two men in deep, we might be able to make something of this. Data, you stay back and do what you have to do."

"Yes, sir."

The chance came a couple of minutes later. Data had the puck hard against the boards in the Owls' end, and both forecheckers converged on him, convinced they could cause a turnover. Instead of panicking, however, Data used the boards to send a long curling pass around to Nish, who picked up the puck in full stride.

As the two forecheckers peeled away from Data, he "slipped" and fell, spinning into one of them and slipping his stick under the other forward's skate. The skate skittered on the stick and the forward slipped to one knee, losing a valuable second.

Nish was already free and flying. He had the puck on the end of his stick and was cutting across centre on the diagonal, looking for the pass to Dmitri. But Dmitri had headed for the bench, and Simon had already leapt over the boards.

Nish saw Simon coming into the play. He faked a forward pass to Sarah, causing the one Selects defenceman to cross over, then dumped a little backhand pass to Simon just as he hit the blueline. With the defenceman already committed to Sarah, he couldn't turn back in time, and Simon was in, alone.

Simon tried the same play – five hole – again, but this time the goaltender was expecting it. She kicked out the rebound hard.

It slid straight into Travis's feet. He turned his right skate and trapped the puck, kicking it ahead onto his stick blade. As he did so, he turned, realizing the crease was suddenly filling up with bodies. There was only one passing option open to him. *Nish.*

The big Owls defenceman was charging the net. Thanks to Data's "accident," there was still no one on Nish. Travis's pass hit Nish perfectly.

The two defencemen tried to converge on Nish, but suddenly Simon spurted through an opening and brushed against the right one so he spun off to the side. By looking back and appearing to be expecting another pass, Simon had made it look accidental. It might have been.

The other defence tackled Nish. He knew he might take a penalty but, given the time in the game and the score, it was his only play. He leapt at Nish, draping himself over him as Nish tried to bull the puck in toward the Selects' net.

Nish wouldn't go down. The Selects defender wrestled him, but Nish broke one hand free as the puck slid between his checker's skates. He shook off the checker, but was in so close he couldn't quite get his stick past the sliding goaltender and the defenceman's back skate.

Nish had no option. Off balance, on the verge of falling into the net, unable even to see exactly what he was doing, he put the stick between his own legs, tried a blind shot, and fell.

The puck rose without enough force to reach the crossbar. It clipped off the goalie's right shoulder, then rolled up and over – and in!

Nish had scored!

And he had scored on the Mario Lemieux between-the-legs shot!

Final score: Owls 3, Selects 2.

The Owls' bench burst open and they flew onto the ice. In the Selects' end, they piled onto Nish, who was yelling and screaming as if he were still on the Tower of Terror ride. Sarah had both arms around Nish. Nish had an arm around Simon, twisting his helmet again. Data piled in, and then came the players from the bench as the cheers poured down on them from the seats of the Ice Palace.

"*We won!*"

"*We won!*"

"*We won!*"

"*You did it, Nish!*" Simon called from the pack. "*You scored on the Lemieux shot!*"

Nish grinned. "Thanks to you, pal."

"How'd you even see it?" Travis asked.

Nish grinned again.

"X-ray vision," he said.

The teams and coaches lined up to shake hands – Muck and his old friend Deke Larose hugging each other – and then they stood for the Canadian anthem.

Travis stood staring up at the Maple Leaf and the American Stars and Stripes. He thought about everything that had happened to the Owls this week. He thought about what might have happened if Data hadn't wondered why the two Goofy costumes were different. He thought about what he would do when he got to the dressing room. He would present Simon with the photograph of him on the ride that had terrified him. After tonight's game, no one would ever again be calling him "Chicken Milliken." Not after what he had done to set up Nish's spectacular goal.

The anthem ended, and a man with dark hair hurried out onto the ice, reaching for Nish, who was trying to get his hands on the trophy. The man pulled Nish aside, and Travis could see him speaking fast to Nish. Nish was nodding, smiling.

The man and Nish began leaving the ice, passing right in front of Travis as they left.

"It's Spanish radio," said Nish. "You were right. They wanted me at the end of the game!"

THE END

THE NEXT BOOK IN THE SCREECH OWLS SERIES

The Quebec City Crisis

The Screech Owls are in Quebec City for the famous Quebec Peewee Invitational. This is the tournament where Guy Lafleur, Wayne Gretzky, and Mario Lemieux first showed the world their incredible talents – and now it's the turn of Travis, Nish, Sarah, and their friends.

But the dream trip soon turns into a nightmare. Travis is asked to keep a diary that will be published in one of the big daily newspapers – and a terrible misunderstanding follows. Soon after Travis's words appear in print, the crowds are booing the Screech Owls, and someone – no one knows who – begins a reign of terror against the team.

The Owls know they are good enough to make it to the tournament final. Sarah could even equal the tournament record set by the great Guy Lafleur! But if the Owls are to stand any chance at all, they must first find out who is trying to destroy them.

The Quebec City Crisis, *the seventh book in* Screech Owls Series, *will be published by McClelland & Stewart in the spring of 1998.*